THE FIVE ANCESTORS

虎 Tiger

Jeff Stone

W9-BRV-875

A YEARLING BOOK

for Jeanie, forever and always.
And then some.

Published by Yearling, an imprint of Random House Children's Books
a division of Random House, Inc., New York

Visit us on the Web! www.randomhouse.com/kids

www.fiveancestors.com

Educators and librarians, for a variety of teaching tools, visit us at
www.randomhouse.com/teachers

ISBN: 0-375-83072-3

Reprinted by arrangement with Random House Children's Books

Printed in the United States of America

March 2006

10 9 8 7 6 5 4 3 2 1

OPM

The Legend . . .

When China's Cangzhen Temple is destroyed, only five young warrior monks survive. Each is named after an animal—tiger, monkey, snake, crane, dragon—for each is the youngest-ever master of that animal's fighting style. The five scatter and begin teaching not only their formidable fighting skills but also their peaceful philosophy of life. It is said that today's martial arts come from the teachings of these five young warrior monks, who are known in legend as . . .

the Five Ancestors.

HENAN PROVINCE, CHINA
4348—YEAR OF THE TIGER
(1650 AD)

"This is stupid," Fu mumbled from the bottom of the terra-cotta barrel. "How long do we have to stay inside this thing? I feel like a pickled vegetable."

"Shhh!" warned his brother Malao, lying directly on top of him. "Grandmaster told us to remain perfectly quiet, and perfectly still."

"I *know* what Grandmaster said," Fu replied. "But we can't stay crammed in here forever. I say we get out right now. I say we stop hiding and fight!"

"Calm yourself, Fu," whispered his brother Seh from on top of Malao. "We are all just as cramped and uncomfortable as you are. But we must do as Grandmaster said and remain silent and hidden. The enemy within our walls is unlike any faced by

Cangzhen Temple in more than a thousand years."

"Yeah, yeah," Fu said. "Stop being so dramatic. You guys are sounding more and more like Grandmaster every day. I don't care who's out there. We're all masters now. We've all passed the tests. We shouldn't be hiding like a bunch of girls. We should be—"

"Hush!" snapped Fu's brother Hok, who was lying on top of Seh. "That's enough, Fu! You're making even *me* angry now."

"I don't care!" Fu replied. "If you think—"

"Quiet!" hissed Fu's oldest brother, Long, from the top of the pile. "Control your tongues, all of you! Brother Fu, empty the words from your mouth and then empty your mind. You must take control of your thoughts and your emotions, or they will control you."

"*You must take control of your thoughts and your emotions, or they will control you,*" Fu mocked. "Give me a break, Long. Right now we need action, not philosophy."

Fu was quickly losing his patience. He could hear enemy horses racing up and down the brick pathways that crisscrossed the temple grounds. He also heard weapons clashing and men crying out—plus a terrible, new sound. It was almost like thunder, except every boom was followed by a pain-filled scream. Fu's keen ears recognized each and every scream. Warrior monks were falling.

A low growl resonated deep within Fu's chest. He didn't understand why his four brothers, stacked above him in the barrel, were holding back. Like him, each had mastered a style of animal kung fu that reflected both his personality and his body type. In fact, their true natures were so perfectly matched with their kung fu styles that they were each named after the animal they mirrored. They were born to fight. But they wouldn't.

Fu, the tiger, growled again. His brothers didn't look like him, walk like him, talk like him, or even smell like him. And they certainly didn't think like him. He called them "brothers" because they all were Buddhist and lived in the temple together. In reality, he and his "brothers" were orphans. What Fu needed were real brothers. Brothers who would fight alongside him.

Fu grunted under the weight of the others. "I can't believe we are just going to—"

"Please!" Long interrupted. "No more talking! We *all* have to remain silent. Brother Fu, focus your breathing. Meditate like the rest of us have been doing. If you find that you cannot meditate, just lie still and relax."

"That's easy for you to say," Fu replied. "You're on top. Try lying down here at the bottom of the pile in a pool of water with Malao's nasty feet pressing up against your lips."

Malao giggled softly and wiggled his toes.

"If you do that again, Malao, I'll bite them off one at a time," Fu said. "I swear I will."

Malao giggled again but kept his toes still.

How much longer am I going to be stuck in here? Fu wondered. He hoped for his brothers' sake they would all get out of the barrel soon. He wasn't sure if he could control himself much longer.

CHAPTER 2

Twelve-year-old Fu couldn't believe his bad luck. He wished he could set the water clock back one hour to the time when Grandmaster first woke him.

Like every night, Fu had been sleeping in the small room he shared with his four brothers at the back of the main sleeping quarters. They had long since retired for the night, and Fu was dreaming about an overflowing banquet table that stretched as far as the eye could see. He'd been about to fill his bowl with a piece of chicken when he was awakened by a smack on the head.

Had the strike come from anyone other than Grandmaster himself, Fu would surely have sprung from his bed and returned the greeting tenfold.

However, Fu instantly recognized Grandmaster's skinny, bald head and orange robe.

Grandmaster grabbed the collar of Fu's robe and yanked him to his feet.

"Rise, now!" Grandmaster whispered into Fu's ear. "We have very little time. Follow your brothers on cat's feet. Go!"

Fu scanned the room with a quick twist of his head. All the beds were empty. His eyes locked on the back door as a small figure scampered outside.

"GO!" Grandmaster urged. He shoved Fu toward the door.

In one great bound, Fu launched himself through the open door and landed silently in the moonlit courtyard. Filling his lungs with the damp night air, Fu raced after his little brother, Malao, who was scurrying around the back corner of the practice hall. By the time Fu reached the enormous wooden doors at the front of the hall, Grandmaster had already caught up with him. Fu's brothers Long, Hok, Seh, and Malao stood there, waiting.

Grandmaster glanced around, then pushed one of the giant doors open just enough to stick his wrinkled head inside. After a moment, he pulled his head back out and looked at Fu. Fu knew exactly what Grandmaster wanted. As Grandmaster opened the door wider, Fu rocked back on his heels and sprang through the doorway.

Fu hit the ancient brick floor without making a sound and rolled to one side. He crouched low and pushed his back flat against the cold stone wall. Like a wary feline, Fu scanned the immense room with his low-light vision. It was empty.

Fu grunted and the others filed in. Grandmaster came last, closing the door behind him.

"Follow me," Grandmaster whispered. "Do not open any shutters. Do not light any torches. If you concentrate, you can see well enough."

"What's going on?" Seh whispered as they moved forward.

"Troops have gathered outside our walls," Grandmaster said. "You are to remain hidden here until I return."

"Troops?" Hok said. "You mean soldiers? Cangzhen is a *secret* temple. How do they know about us?"

"I fear they are led by your lost brother, Ying," Grandmaster replied.

"Ying!" Fu growled. "He's no longer my brother! Where is he? I'll tear him to shreds!"

"No, you won't," Malao said, giggling. "Ying's eagle kung fu is much too powerful for you. Remember the time he broke your arm because you woke him up?"

"Watch it, Malao," Fu replied.

Malao skipped forward, still giggling. "And remember the time he tied you to that tree with his chain whip? Right beneath that big hornet's nest!"

"Stop it," Fu said, pivoting toward Malao. "I'm warning you—"

Malao giggled louder. "Oh! And remember the time he—"

"That's enough, you two," Long whispered as he positioned his muscular body between Fu and Malao. Malao stopped giggling.

"Us *two*?" Fu said, irritated. "I didn't even—"

"I said, *enough*!" Long hissed. Fu glared at Long but kept his mouth shut. Long turned toward Grandmaster. "Pardon me for asking, Grandmaster, but you think Ying is leading the troops? How can this be? He is only sixteen years old."

"Never underestimate anyone," Grandmaster said. "Especially Ying. He is very cunning. Now, of this matter I will say no more, and neither will any of you. You will remain silent."

When they reached the far wall of the practice hall, Grandmaster motioned for them to stop while he continued off to one side. As soon as Grandmaster's footfalls grew too faint to hear, Fu whispered, "I wonder if Ying has come to steal the secret dragon scrolls. He swore he'd come back and—"

"Quiet!" whispered Long.

"Shhh!" whispered Seh.

"Fine," whispered Fu, and he turned away from the group.

Across the room a sliver of moonlight was sneaking through a crack in one of the shutters. It shined against the far wall, illuminating the face of Fu's favorite character in his favorite mural. Of the hundreds of life-size instructional fighting scenes covering every wall inside the dark practice hall, this beam had chosen to shine on the heavyset monk striking an opponent with a devastating tiger-claw swipe.

It must be a sign, Fu thought. It reminded him that he and his brothers were full-fledged warrior monks—Cangzhen Temple's youngest ever. Each of them had mastered a different animal style by age eleven. It took most people twice that long.

Fu didn't know what made them so special, and he didn't really care. The only thing he wondered about occasionally was their peculiar names, which Grandmaster had given them as infants. Though they mainly spoke Mandarin Chinese—the same dialect everyone in the region used—for some reason Grandmaster had selected their names in a Chinese dialect called Cantonese. Whatever the reason, Grandmaster knew what he was doing. *Fu* meant "tiger" in Cantonese. And, like the monk in the mural, Fu was a tiger, through and through.

Fu had a large, round head, which was clean-shaven and accented by small ears and sharp, challenging eyes. His voice was deep and gravelly and, just like his animal counterpart, he was very aggressive and unusually short-tempered. Though Fu was the second youngest of the five and not exactly tall, he was by far the largest and strongest. His arms were as big as most of his brothers' legs, and his legs were as big as a man's. Fu was solid and thick from lifting stone weights and generous of width from lifting his rice bowl.

It came as no surprise, then, when Grandmaster

quietly called them over to the back corner of the practice hall and told them that Fu would be the first to climb into the terra-cotta barrel that held drinking water more often than it held boys.

Grandmaster removed the barrel's heavy lid and, groaning softly, dumped the contents onto the floor. Fu felt the water splash onto his pants and knee-length robe, then spill over his bare feet. He hated to wear wet clothes, so he took several steps back—but Grandmaster shook his head.

Grandmaster quickly stood the barrel back up and nodded in Fu's direction. Fu growled softly and stepped forward. He laid his hands on the rim of the barrel and found it to be quite stable, so he swung himself up and into it feetfirst like he was jumping into a well. And just like jumping into a well, he found water at the bottom.

"What the . . . ?" Fu complained. "There's still a bunch of water in here! What do you expect me to do?"

Grandmaster slapped Fu's bald head. "I expect you to stop talking and lie down! Hurry! Curl into a tight ball and lie on your side."

Fu grudgingly did as he was told but found that much of his head would be under water if he followed Grandmaster's directions exactly. Instead, Fu twisted his head to one side and rested his cheek on the inside wall of the barrel.

"I can't believe this," Fu mumbled. "Whoever gets on top of me better—"

"Hush!" Grandmaster said. He looked anxiously at Fu's four brothers standing around the barrel in the gloom. Three of them avoided Grandmaster's gaze. Malao, however, flashed a devilish grin and leaped high into the air. Grandmaster frowned but did nothing to stop the eleven-year-old "monkey."

Malao's bare, dark-skinned feet landed directly on Fu's head, and he began to giggle as he flopped down on top of Fu. Malao was the smallest of the group and didn't weigh very much, but Fu complained anyway. Grandmaster sighed and looked at Seh.

Without a word, Seh, the serious twelve-year-old "snake," stretched his long, sinewy arms straight up into the air and slid his lanky body over the barrel's rim. Malao stopped giggling after Seh entered the barrel. Fu, however, complained even more when he felt the added weight of his tallest brother pressing down on him.

Hok, the quiet twelve-year-old "crane," followed Seh without being prompted. His body was of average size, but he was incredibly light. He hopped directly onto the rim of the barrel. Perfectly balanced on the balls of both feet, he leaned forward and stretched his delicate neck to peer inside. After studying the pile a few moments, he gently lowered his pale body into the barrel.

Long, the wise thirteen-year-old "dragon," went last. He wasn't as strong as Fu, as nimble as Malao, as smooth as Seh, or as gentle as Hok, but he was very, very close in each regard. He placed his large hands on the rim of the barrel like Fu and swung his powerful legs high into the air. But instead of rushing in heavy-footed like Malao, Long quickly checked the positions of the others like Hok had done. While still in midair, Long's muscular, rock-solid body became fluid like a snake, and he wriggled himself down gently into what little space was left at the top of the pile.

Grandmaster finished the job by replacing the barrel's heavy lid. Only then did Fu stop complaining.

But Fu was ready to start complaining all over again. Just when he thought things couldn't get any worse inside the barrel, they did. His brothers were beginning to smell. They were all wearing their cold-weather robes and pants, which made them sweat profusely inside the cramped space. Even their bald heads and bare feet were sweating.

On top of Fu, Malao shifted one of his slimy feet. A dirty toenail poked Fu in the eye. Fu growled and Malao's foot returned to its original position.

Fu wondered what he had done in a former life to deserve this. He was wet and uncomfortable at the bottom of the barrel, and half his body had fallen asleep under the weight of the others. Worst of all, he was being forced to listen to a battle being waged in his own backyard while he lay there, doing nothing.

Fu grumbled to himself. If he hadn't been half-asleep, he would never have agreed to this. Especially with Ying involved.

If you're not part of the solution, you're part of the

problem, Fu thought. Ying, of all people, had told him that.

I've got to get out of this stupid barrel! Fu decided.

Fu began to shake as he struggled to restrain himself. Expressing his thoughts like a civilized person hadn't gotten him anywhere, so he decided to take a different approach. He would muscle his way out. All he needed was a little leverage. Maybe if he were to shift his left shoulder back a little . . . *errr* . . . And then push his right arm forward a little . . . *arrr* . . . And then turn his head a little to the . . . *SLAM!*

Fu's head was unexpectedly pinned to the bottom of the barrel by Malao's foot. Fu couldn't believe the little monkey would be so bold! He opened his mouth to give Malao a piece of his mind, but instead of sound coming out, a flood of water rushed in.

CHAPTER
3

"**M**ajor Ying, be careful!" shouted an armor-clad soldier. He sprinted toward Cangzhen Temple's practice hall, leaping over lifeless bodies and fallen horses.

Ying stopped short of the practice hall's huge wooden doors and turned toward the running soldier. A flurry of flaming arrows suddenly filled the night sky and rained down onto the green tiles covering the stone building's elaborate wooden roof. The soldier dove behind a dead horse as arrows bounced off the tiles and went careening into the surrounding courtyard. They sliced into anything—alive or dead—that wasn't wearing armor.

Ying, who never wore armor, didn't budge.

"Please step away from the hall, sir!" the soldier pleaded from behind the horse. "Arrows will continue to fly from the compound's perimeter, and you're unprotected."

Ying stood firm, his blood-streaked silk robe clinging to tight, sinewy muscles as he folded his arms. A burning arrow flashed overhead and took root above him in one of the roof's ornate, up-curved corners. The flickering flames illuminated his face.

The soldier shuddered.

"Come over here," Ying said in a steady voice. "Now!"

The soldier hesitated, then ran up to Ying and dropped to his knees. He removed his helmet and kowtowed three times to show his respect, knocking his forehead against the dusty ground with each bow.

"Rise," said Ying, glaring at the man. "I see this building is the last to be burned. Has it been fully searched?"

"It has, sir," the soldier said as he stood. His eyes remained glued to the ground. "I searched it myself. The only thing inside is an empty water barrel."

"How do you know the barrel is empty?" Ying asked.

"Because I saw water on the floor, sir."

"Was the barrel laying on its side?"

"No, sir. But . . ." The soldier's voice trailed off.

"But what?" asked Ying in a low voice.

The soldier squeezed his eyes shut and began to tremble.

"I think I see your point, sir," the soldier replied. "There could be someone hiding inside the barrel."

"That's right," said Ying, popping his knuckles one at a time. "In fact, there could be *several* someones hiding inside it. Warrior monks are quite flexible, you know."

"A—a thousand pardons, Major Ying," the soldier stammered, his eyes still clamped shut. "I have failed you. I will not fail you again. Please be generous and give me one more chance to prove myself worthy of your esteemed command."

"What do you suggest?" Ying asked.

The soldier turned away from Ying and opened his eyes. He stared at the practice hall as a second wave of flaming arrows arched overhead. Two of the arrows sank into the upper reaches of one of the giant doors, setting it aflame. The soldier swallowed hard and cast his eyes down once more.

"I will reenter this practice hall and investigate, sir," the soldier said. "Though I am certain there is no one left to flush out."

Ying leaned in close to the soldier, popping his last knuckle. "What makes you so certain?"

"Because the reports indicate that all one hundred monks have been killed, sir."

"Must I also include mathematics in our military training programs, you half-wit!" Ying shrieked. Like an angry beast, he bared his teeth and his face contorted. "Look at me when I'm talking to you!"

With lightning speed, Ying snapped his hand back

and formed a perfect eagle claw by bringing his extended fingers together and curling them down while rotating his thumb down and curling it up. He thrust the open claw into the soldier's lowered face, latching on forcefully with four fingertips above the soldier's eyebrows and his thumb below the soldier's chin. Ying flicked his wrist powerfully upward, forcing the soldier's face up as well. His long fingernails pierced the soldier's skin, and he ripped his hand away with a brutal, flesh-stripping twist.

"Now think!" Ying said, leaning into the soldier's face. "I've informed everyone in our camp several times that one hundred monks call this their home—*along with their Grandmaster and five boys.*"

"I see, sir," squeaked the soldier, blinking furiously as four streams of blood ran down his forehead, into his eyes. "There should be one hundred six bodies. Thank you very much for the lesson, Major Ying. I've heard no reports of a Grandmaster or boys, so perhaps this is their hiding place. I will take my *qiang* with me into that hall. I think I have a plan."

"Excellent," said Ying, leaning back. "Now, I must warn you—if you are not out in the time it takes to drink half a cup of tea, I am coming in. Do you understand what *that* means, half-wit?"

"C-c-completely, sir."

"Good. Then there is just one more thing. Those boys are not ordinary boys. I suggest you watch yourself around them."

"Watch myself, sir?" the soldier asked hesitantly,

struggling to keep his burning, blood-filled eyes fixed on Ying's hideous face.

"Never mind," Ying said, turning toward the practice hall. "Just get in there before I really lose my temper."

fu was drowning. Malao's foot pinned one entire side of his face against the bottom of the terra-cotta barrel. His mouth and nose were completely under water. Panicking, Fu used what little air he had left to spit out the water that was in his mouth. Denied oxygen, instinct took over. His body jerked and twisted involuntarily.

Malao pressed his foot down even harder.

A small pocket of air had been trapped between Fu's ear and the bottom of the barrel. Malao's added pressure squeezed it out, creating a vacuum. Fu felt his inner ear stick to the smooth bottom of the barrel like a suction cup. Pain shot through his head, jolting his nervous system. Tiny white lights flashed behind his closed eyelids. His head twitched violently, and his mouth flew open in a silent scream. Water rushed into his mouth again.

Above him, Fu heard Malao cry out. Fu felt Malao trying to lift his foot, but it must have been pinned by the weight of the others.

"Hey, guys!" Malao shouted. "We need to get out of here! I think Fu is—"

KAA-BOOM!

Thunder echoed through the practice hall as the barrel holding the five young monks exploded into a thousand pieces. Fu and his brothers were sent rolling across the floor. Jagged terra-cotta shards dug into their backs, sides, legs, and arms. Fu landed on his stomach, and water poured from his open mouth.

Fu took a huge gulp of air. His head pounded, and his ears rang from the blast. He couldn't wait to get his hands on Malao. He shook his head in an effort to clear his senses, and the large room slowly began to take shape.

Unlike the darkness that had surrounded Fu before he climbed into the barrel, an eerie glow now possessed the entire practice hall. Flames danced across the inside of the roof high above, reaching down to embrace the gigantic rafters running the length of the building. Thick black smoke slowly filled the room.

At the entrance, one of the huge doors was ajar and completely engulfed in flames. The monks in the murals near the open door all seemed to be looking in the same direction—the very center of the room. There stood an armor-clad soldier wearing a strange helmet, holding an even stranger weapon. Four streams of blood ran down his face.

Malao would have to wait.

Fu was about to call to his brothers when he heard a yell from overhead. Surprised, he looked up as Grandmaster dropped from one of the rafters. With empty hands, Grandmaster approached the soldier.

The soldier straightened his helmet and adjusted his heavy, flexible body armor, which was made from hundreds of small metal plates. Though he stood his ground confidently, Fu noticed that the soldier seemed uncertain of what he should do with the weapon he held in his hands. It was then that Fu realized the soldier's strange weapon was a *qiang*. Fu had never seen one before, but he had heard about them. This one looked like a metal staff about as long as a man's leg, with a large piece of wood attached to one end. The metal staff appeared to be hollow like bamboo, and white smoke drifted from the end opposite the wood. Fu knew that a great burst of energy threw a ball of lead—or many balls of lead— from the *qiang* with a fantastic *BOOM!* Fu realized that this particular *qiang* must have been responsible for their barrel exploding. He had heard that once a *qiang* was used, it took some time before it could be used again—which must be why the soldier seemed uncertain of what to do with it now.

The soldier grunted and cast the *qiang* aside with

a metallic *CRASH!* Wiping the blood from his eyes, he yanked a large, curved broadsword from a sheath slung across his back. The blade was wide and flexible. It shimmered in the firelight as the man raised the weapon with both hands and ran straight for Grandmaster.

Any concern Fu had for Grandmaster's well-being quickly faded. Whoever was hiding inside that armor might be well protected, but he was most likely not a very good fighter. Only a novice would raise a broadsword high over his head with two hands and rush toward an opponent.

When the soldier was within striking distance, he swung his broadsword downward at an angle, intending to slice Grandmaster in half diagonally. As the blade dropped, however, Grandmaster leaped to one side and delivered a swift knife-hand chop to the back of the soldier's neck. The soldier collapsed onto himself like a rag doll, the metal plates of his armor ringing out like wind chimes.

"Buddha, forgive me," Grandmaster said. He closed his eyes and lowered his head for a moment, then turned to face Fu and the others.

"That was great!" Malao squealed. "When you stepped off to the side and—"

"Silence, Malao!" Grandmaster said. "I know at least a hundred ways to turn a weak fighter like him away with only minor injuries. Instead, I took his life. That was wrong."

Grandmaster shook his head slowly, and Fu

noticed that something wasn't quite right with him. For the first time ever, Grandmaster looked . . . exhausted.

"My judgment is clouding," Grandmaster sighed. "I have fought many men this night, and I have released far too many souls to the heavens. It seems each time I release one, I release a little of myself. I fear my time is coming to an end. . . . Quickly! Everyone! Gather around!"

Long was the first to reach Grandmaster's side.

"What is happening out there, Grandmaster?" Long asked.

"There are many words in the language of men," Grandmaster said, "but none of them can describe the darkness that has descended upon us this night. Brother has turned against brother, and nothing will ever be the same."

Hok stared at Grandmaster, unblinking. "So Ying is involved after all?"

"Yes," Grandmaster said, lowering his head.

"Then where did the troops come from?" Seh asked.

"The Emperor himself, it seems," Grandmaster replied.

"Really?" Malao said, scratching his small, bald head. "The new Emperor is responsible for this attack?"

"No," said Grandmaster, raising his eyes. "I am responsible, for I have failed Ying. I made it my mission years ago to change his heart, and I did not succeed. Now you five must change him."

"I'll change him!" Fu declared. "I'll change him into a corpse for attacking us!"

"No!" Grandmaster said. "Violence accomplishes nothing. In order to truly make a difference you must find a noble way to change Ying. The Emperor must change, too, for his heart seems to be as black as Ying's."

"But how can we change them, Grandmaster?" Long asked.

"I do not know," Grandmaster replied. "My own methods were not successful. Perhaps the answer lies in the past. In your past, as well as Ying's. As you know, all of you are orphans. So is Ying. All six of you are special because you have extraordinary kung fu skills. What you do not know is that your pasts are firmly linked. Ying is obsessed with the past. That is why he has returned."

"What?" Fu said. "I thought Ying returned to steal the secret dragon scrolls. He swore he would come back to get them."

"This is also true," Grandmaster said. "Ying is an eagle, but he yearns to be an all-powerful dragon. However, I do not think the scrolls will be enough. Ying has a hole in his life, and he holds me responsible for it. He is a vengeful soul. He will not stop until everything that is important to me is gone. Even after I myself am gone."

Grandmaster paused, looking Fu and each of Fu's brothers in the eye. "Cangzhen matters most to me, and you five matter most to Cangzhen. That is why you were hidden. You are Cangzhen's future, but I fear Ying will not stop until he has destroyed all of you. You must change him before he succeeds."

"You want us to change him?" Fu challenged. "Ying is going to try to kill us for something we didn't even do, and you want us to *change* him? Why don't we just kill him first?"

"No!" Grandmaster said. "Your pasts are interwoven with Ying's, and so are your futures. You must not kill him."

"But—"

"Enough!" Long interrupted. "Brother Fu, we don't have time to argue. We need to make a plan. Please, bite your tongue—until it bleeds, if necessary."

Fu growled. Long ignored him.

"Grandmaster," Long said, "you mentioned that the troops were the Emperor's. Why would the Emperor help Ying destroy Cangzhen? We just saved the Emperor's life and his throne last year."

"I can only guess," Grandmaster replied, looking up at the burning rafters. "But we have no more time for discussion. You must leave now. Scatter into the four winds and uncover Ying's secrets, as well as your own. Uncover the past, for it is your future. Your burden is great, my young monks. May Buddha bless you."

"I'm not going anywhere!" Fu announced.

"Don't be foolish, Fu," Grandmaster said. "Ying

will count the dead and realize you are not among them. He will then come looking for you. All of you must run."

"I refuse to run!" Fu roared. "I will stay and fight! Let's take care of Ying now!"

"Fu, listen to me!" Grandmaster urged. "Ying and his men are too powerful. We monks are defenseless against their *qiang*s. One hundred Cangzhen deaths prove that."

"What!" Fu cried. "No!"

"Hear me now!" Grandmaster said. "Hearts grow dark quickly in these times. Do not open your heart to this loss or it will fill you up. It will consume you. Let it go, Fu. Run, and don't look back."

"I CAN'T!"

"You must! All of you must. You are all that is left. Now go! Seek out pure hearts and teach them the ways of Cangzhen. You will need help, for there is much work to be done."

Grandmaster looked directly at Fu.

"Always remember, you represent Cangzhen. Do not accept any offers of violence—but do not accept any delivery of harm, either. Fight if you must, but only in defense. And respond with as little violence as possible. I ask that you honor me with that."

Fu glared at Grandmaster. Grandmaster sighed and shook his head.

Suddenly Grandmaster's entire body stiffened and he turned toward the practice hall's entry. The smoke inside was much thicker now, and Fu could no longer see all the way to the entry doors. But he thought he heard something. Yes. It was faint and growing louder. It was the sound of . . . claws? Yes! Claws scraping steadily against the brick floor as something approached.

A tall, slender figure appeared, striding confidently forward. His head and shoulders were obscured by smoke, but Fu could see that he wore no armor. He held a *qiang* across his body with both hands and wore the formal uniform of the new Emperor: a red silk sash bound a green long-sleeve silk robe at the waist. Beneath, he wore red silk pants. All were blood-streaked.

As the intruder drew closer, Fu saw that his feet were bare. He had extraordinarily long toenails that curved savagely downward. Filed into sharp points, they scraped the brick floor like talons.

The man took a few more steps, and Fu saw black hair that was short and in disarray. Fu caught a glimpse of the stranger's intense eyes and contracted every muscle in his entire body, like a large cat ready to pounce.

But when his lost brother, Ying, was finally close enough to be seen in full, Fu shrank back on his haunches.

CHAPTER 5

Sixteen-year-old Ying stopped several paces from Fu. His black eyes sparkled as Fu and the others stared.

Deep grooves had been chiseled into Ying's face and filled with dark green pigment. They resembled heavy folds of reptilian skin. Thick furrows stretched from the corners of Ying's mouth to the top of his jaw and horizontally across his forehead. Intricate scales had also been carved from ear to ear and hairline to chin. They, too, were filled with pigment.

Ying curled back his lips, revealing perfect white teeth, each of which had been ground to a sharp point. Fu's eyes widened as Ying flicked his tongue forward. It was extraordinarily long and separated into two distinct segments at the tip. The right half flexed upward while the left half went down. Ying repeated the exercise in reverse before returning his forked tongue to its normal position. He laughed as Fu continued to stare.

Ying shifted the *qiang* in his hands. A glint of firelight reflected off the weapon's metal barrel, and Fu noticed that Ying's fingernails, like the nails on his grotesque, clawlike feet, were extraordinarily long and filed sharp. Bits of bloodstained flesh dangled from their tips. Fu looked at Grandmaster out of the corner of his eye and felt some of his initial shock begin to fade. Grandmaster was gazing at Ying through the thickening smoke with only pity in his eyes.

Ying cleared his throat and looked at Fu.

"Hello, boys," he said casually. "Or should I say girls? I had a feeling you would all be hiding like a bunch of females."

Fu locked eyes with Ying. He released a low growl.

"Stay calm, Sister Fu," Ying said, smiling. "I won't bite. At least not just yet."

Fu growled again and tensed his whole body in preparation for an attack. Hok drifted over to his side and placed a hand on his shoulder.

"Relax, Fu," Hok said. "I understand your urge to attack. But you must resist. Ying is only throwing words at you, not daggers. He is up to something. I can feel it."

"The birdbrain speaks!" Ying announced. "Fu, this must be serious. Hok rarely utters a peep. Maybe I really *am* up to something."

"Who are you to call Hok birdbrain?" Fu snarled. "You're an eagle!"

"Do I look like an eagle to you?" Ying asked.

"You look like a fool," Fu replied.

Ying opened his mouth wide and hissed at Fu. He flicked out his tongue and flexed its tip.

"What are you going to do with that?" Fu asked. "Lick me to death?"

Ying slipped his tongue back into his mouth and spat on the floor. He took a step toward Fu, and Fu roared. Every muscle in Fu's body began to shake.

Hok lifted his hand from Fu's shoulder and took a step back.

"Aren't you precious?" Ying scowled at Fu. "Purring like a little kitten. Would you like me to scratch behind your cute little ears?"

Fu could contain himself no longer. He sprang at Ying's throat with his teeth bared and arms out-stretched. Ying dropped the *qiang* and repositioned himself to intercept Fu.

But Fu never reached Ying. Fu gasped and doubled over in midair as Grandmaster's narrow, bony shoulder struck him square in the diaphragm. Fu hit the ground flat on his back with a loud *THUD*, the wind completely knocked out of him. Grandmaster rolled over Fu's chest and whispered, "The pain you feel now is *nothing* compared to what you will feel if Ying gets his hands on you. You cannot defeat him alone. His kung fu is too powerful. This time you will listen to what I say! You will stay back! I will handle this."

Fu wheezed and hacked as he sucked air, struggling to reclaim his breath for the second time that night. He nodded his head.

Grandmaster stood and spun around to face Ying.

Ying grinned. He bent down and picked up the *qiang*.

"My dear old man," Ying said. "How could you be so cruel to that poor little kitten?"

Fu lifted himself onto his hands and knees. He glared at Ying.

Grandmaster said nothing.

"If you ask me, I think that was precious," Ying said. "It was almost worth him escaping my grasp to see the fearless giant of a tiger boy knocked down by a brittle old toothpick of a monk. Aaah . . . no matter, I'll snap his fat neck soon enough."

Grandmaster remained silent.

"Oh, come now," Ying said. "Your eldest prodigy has just returned after being gone nearly a year. Don't you have anything to say?"

"I am sorry I have failed you, Ying," Grandmaster said. Fu thought he saw tears forming in Grandmaster's eyes.

"Oh, *now* you're sorry," Ying said. "After I've destroyed nearly everything you care about—just like you've destroyed everything I care about. It's a little late to apologize, don't you think?"

Grandmaster said nothing.

Ying scowled. "You haven't changed one bit, old man. Somebody asks you a question, and you respond with a blank stare. *Like a stupid child,* as the Emperor would say. You know, you could have learned a thing or two from him last year, but you decided to leave his palace. Why?"

"Because our job was complete," Grandmaster replied.

"Was it?" Ying said. "The Emperor asked us to stay and serve as his full-time protectors. He was going to pay us with *gold.* But you refused his generous offer. You even refused to accept the gold he offered as payment for what we had already done. Why?"

"We are monks, not bodyguards or warriors for hire," Grandmaster replied.

"Then why did we go there in the first place?" Ying asked. "You made me and thirty other Cangzhen monks risk our lives to save him and his throne. One of us didn't make it back because of you! What was the point? What was our reward?"

"Your success was our reward," Grandmaster said calmly.

"And what did we gain from that success?" Ying asked. "I know for a fact you do not approve of the Emperor."

"This is true," Grandmaster said. "But our efforts saved our region from someone far worse than the new Emperor."

"Who are you to judge that one man is worse than another?" Ying shouted. "Your decisions are foolhardy! You should have taken the gold. *Everything* would be different if you had. My best friend would still be alive, and so would all your monks!"

Grandmaster said nothing.

"Fool! When I take that blank stare of yours to the Emperor with your head attached, my reward will be the title General. Then *I* will make all the decisions in this region you've secretly influenced for so long. What do you think of that, old man?"

Grandmaster stared back, silent.

Ying spat and turned to face Long.

"What do *you* think, Dragon Boy?"

Long paused, and Fu saw the same pity in his eyes that he saw in Grandmaster's. Long folded his hands as if in prayer and said, "Though I share your grief for the brother we lost, Ying, I think you disgust me."

"My sincerest apologies for having turned your stomach, dear brother," Ying replied sarcastically. "I realize my appearance is quite striking."

"You misunderstand," Long said, unfolding his hands. "It is your motivations that disgust me. Your appearance is simply ridiculous."

"That's right," Seh added, walking over to Long's side. "Grandmaster always said you would catch the eyes of the girls if you ever left Cangzhen. That is certainly true now. An eagle with a lizard's head is absurd."

"I have very little eagle left in me, blind fools," Ying said, spreading his arms wide. His bloody silk robe glistened in the smoky firelight. "I have changed quite a lot since you saw me last, and soon my transformation will be complete. My number one man is gathering the dragon scrolls as we speak. I am confident I will learn the ancient dragon arts in no time."

Fu looked over at Grandmaster and saw him shaking his head slowly.

"You are no dragon, Ying," Grandmaster said. "To be a dragon, you must first be wise. You are certainly clever, but being wise and being clever are two very different things. You would be far better off stealing the secret eagle scrolls and learning from them instead. Perhaps they would guide you onto the right path. I might consider allowing you to take them with my blessing."

"Ha!" Ying said. "You offer me things I can take at will. Perhaps you should have offered them to me before you destroyed my world. No matter, your gifts are surely worthless by now. I have instructed my man to take the dragon scrolls and burn everything else in the library."

Fu saw Grandmaster stiffen. Hok began to shift from foot to foot, anxiously bobbing his head up and down. Fu couldn't see Malao, but Long and Seh stood still as stone, staring coldly at Ying.

What's going on? Fu wondered. Then it hit him. Those scrolls were the only source of information for further training for them—or for anyone else. The library contained advanced scrolls for every kung fu style imaginable, holding a thousand times more information than could fit even inside Grandmaster's head. Without those scrolls, their kung fu might disappear. Forever.

"Hey, Lizard Face," Fu called out as he stood up. "Why would you burn all the other scrolls?"

"I have no interest in them," Ying replied casually.

Long's eyes narrowed. "You would destroy one thousand years of history simply because you did not find it of interest?"

"Absolutely," Ying replied.

"That is most unwise," Long said in a solemn tone. "A dragon you will never be."

Fu watched Ying's carved face grow dark. Ying shouldered his *qiang* and pointed it at Long.

"Enough of this idle talk!" Ying shouted. "When you are gone, Brother Long, *I* will be the last dragon!"

"That is not true," Grandmaster interrupted. "For I, too, am a dragon."

Ying turned the *qiang* toward Grandmaster.

"Thank you for reminding me," Ying said. "I nearly forgot. I shall kill you first, then. It seems most fitting, anyway, that you—the *old* man—should be on the receiving end of my *new* weapon."

Grandmaster paused. Fu assumed he was taking a moment to analyze the *qiang* so that he could figure out how to counter it.

"Your toy does not concern me," Grandmaster said. "What harm can come from a hollow metal staff?"

Ying laughed. "A hollow metal staff? Is that all you see? This weapon is the future. With a single finger, someone who's never trained in the fighting arts can destroy a warrior monk with sixty years of training!"

Ying waved a finger at Grandmaster as if scolding him. His voice lowered. "There is no defense against this weapon, you sneaky old man, so stop trying to figure one out."

Fu saw Grandmaster smirk as the old man's voice boomed, "My young monks, when I count to three, run for the door!

"ONE!"

Ying took aim.

"TWO!"

KAA-BOOM!

There was an explosion of light and sound as Ying fired the *qiang* at Grandmaster's chest.

But Grandmaster was no longer there. The instant Ying's finger began to move beneath the *qiang,* Grandmaster had hit the ground and rolled toward Ying. Grandmaster lashed out with a vicious leg swipe.

Before Ying even hit the floor, Grandmaster yelled, "THREE! RUN!"

CHAPTER
6

The young monks ran. Hok sailed through the flame-filled doorway first. Seh followed, quick as a whip, with Malao scampering close behind. Fu bounded powerfully through the flames, and Long zipped outside last, fast as lightning.

After just a few strides, Long was out front, leading the others through the smoky darkness toward the Hall of a Thousand Buddhas. Fu thought they should head in the opposite direction, but he knew no one would listen if he protested—so he kept his mouth shut and followed as best he could. His body was built for power, not speed. He had a hard time keeping up.

The scene unfolding before Fu was worse than anything he could have imagined. Flames leaped from every building. In the eerie glow, he could see orange robes everywhere, filled with dead monks. Hundreds of armor-clad soldiers lay flat on their backs with long spears extending straight up into the air from their throats. Fu choked on smoke and the stench of burning bodies that had been ignited by flaming arrows. He wanted revenge so badly now, he could taste it. But he knew he'd be of no use to himself or anyone else if he were dead. He picked up his pace as best he could.

Fu made it to the back door of the Thousand Buddhas hall only a few strides behind the others. He knew what Long was thinking—they would cut through the hall on their way to the main gate. But when Long thrust the door open, burning air rushed out to greet them like a kiss from a dragon. Long jumped back, and Fu heard mortar cracking and bricks exploding inside from the tremendous heat. They would have to take the long way around.

Fu shook his head. He knew they should have gone the other way!

With Long in the lead, they ran once more. They raced along paths of bloodstained bricks, and Fu saw the dining hall, the toilets, the bathhouse, and the library—all burning.

Fu was surprised when they made it through the maze of buildings without encountering any soldiers. He was even more surprised when Long stopped ahead of him at the main gate. The others were stopped, too.

Beyond the gate lay a grassy, moonlit area that separated the walls of the compound from a distant tree line, which was the beginning of a great, mountainous forest. Fu knew this grassy "moat" was kept treeless and well trimmed so that an enemy attacking Cangzhen would have nowhere to hide.

Fu caught up with the group. "What are you doing?" he asked Long, panting heavily. "Why did you stop?"

"There may be soldiers positioned in the tree line," Long replied. "They could shoot us with arrows as we run across the open space, or they could wait and attack us as soon as we reach the trees."

"So?" Malao said. "There are probably soldiers still here on the temple grounds. What else can we do?"

"Malao's right," said Seh. "We have to take our chances over the grass, and then in the forest."

"What does everyone else think?" Long asked the group.

"We should run for the trees," Hok said softly. "And then separate as Grandmaster wished."

"Brother Fu?" Long said.

"I think we should stay and fight!" Fu replied. "If we—"

"Sorry, Fu," Long interrupted. "Fighting is not an option."

"Fighting *back* is an option!" Fu roared.

"Keep your voice down, Fu!" Seh said. He turned toward Long. "Malao, Hok, and I say we should run for the trees. Three is a majority vote. That means we run."

"And then separate," Hok added quietly.

"Then it is decided," Long said, nodding his head. "We must make haste. Goodbye, brothers. We shall meet again."

Without another word, Long turned and ran like the wind across the open expanse. The others raced after him. Pumped full of adrenaline, they reached the tree line at more or less the same time. There were no soldiers there.

Without looking back, Malao, the "monkey," let out a soft, high-pitched screech and took to the treetops. He was gone in the blink of an eye. Seh, the "snake," slipped away through a patch of ferns, low to the ground. Hok, the "crane," glided off into the wind, while Long, the "dragon," seemed to disappear, like the mythical creatures were rumored to do.

Fu, the "tiger," turned to run headlong into the forest, but his feet would not listen. It seemed they were connected to his heart, which was determined to stay and do something.

Fu spotted an enormous tree at the edge of the grassy expanse and clawed his way up as high as his weight would allow. Then he went out on a limb to evaluate the situation.

Back inside the smoke-filled practice hall, student and master stood toe to toe in a fight to the death. Though Ying was covered with battle stains, he had actually fought very little that night. He was young, rested, and extremely quick and strong. Grandmaster was unbelievably quick as well and normally had the strength of ten men. Tonight he alone had fought and defeated more than one hundred soldiers before sneaking back into the practice hall. But the fighting had taken its toll. Grandmaster was weak. He had no secret potions or ancient methods to regain his strength in the blink of an eye. Those things did not exist. He was just a man who had worked very hard and learned many skills in his lifetime.

Ying popped his knuckles one at a time.

"You know the real reason I've returned, don't you, old man?" Ying spat.

"From the look in your eyes, I can tell," Grandmaster replied.

"I hate you!"

"I know."

Chapter 7

Fu lay on his stomach, his arms and legs wrapped tightly around a thick tree limb. He stared down at the Cangzhen compound. Every single building was burning. Fu strained his keen eyes, searching for movement in the smoky moonlight.

Way back in the far-left corner of the compound, small groups of soldiers walked from the weapons shed to the sleeping quarters. *That's where they are,* Fu thought. *But what are they up to?* There were weapons to steal in the shed, but there certainly wasn't anything worth taking in the sleeping quarters.

Then Fu remembered the secret escape tunnel. It stretched underground from the sleeping quarters to beyond the back wall of the compound. It was rigged with numerous traps to stop an enemy from trying to sneak through it. Ying must have disabled the devices. He was one of the few people who knew how. Fu could picture Ying disarming the crossbows armed with poison arrows and unhooking the swinging pendulum blades as his men followed.

Fu growled. He decided that if he couldn't defeat Ying directly, he would hurt him indirectly. Since the soldiers appeared to be leaving through the tunnel, they probably already had the dragon scrolls. Fu decided to retrieve them, no matter what the cost.

Fu leaped down from the tree limb and landed in a silent roll at the forest's edge. Then he ran low to the ground across the grassy expanse back toward Cangzhen's main gate. He made it through the gate without seeing anyone and headed for the bathhouse, which was on the left side of the compound, not too far from the weapons shed. He had seen something there that gave him an idea.

Fu reached the bathhouse undetected and cautiously approached a fallen soldier he'd noticed when he'd run by with his brothers earlier. The soldier was heavyset and about the same size he was. Fu's hand quivered as he reached down to take the man's helmet. He had never been this close to a dead person before. Fu looked away as he laid his hands on the helmet and caught a glimpse of his fallen brother Sing. Sing was an older brother and had taught Fu how to use edged weapons. He was the kindest teacher Fu had ever had.

The dead soldier would have to wait. Fu stood up and headed for Sing.

Sing lay with his favorite pair of tiger hook swords still in his hands. Fu felt tears of hatred and grief well up in his eyes, but he did not let them fall. Instead of crying, he would do something. In life, those tiger hook swords had meant everything to Sing. They were an extension of his body as well as his soul. Fu would honor Sing's spirit by keeping the spirit of his weapons alive. He took the paired swords from his brother's cold hands.

Fu inspected the weapons quickly as he walked back to the dead soldier. Except for some fresh bloodstains on the silk handle wraps, the tiger hook swords were in perfect shape. Both sides of the long, straight, double-edged swords were razor-sharp, and the large hook on the end of each sword resembling a tiger's claw showed no signs of fatigue. The crescent-shaped hand-guard daggers were also still sharp, as were the single daggers that protruded from the bottom of each sword's handle. Sing's tiger hook swords were perfectly weighted and felt powerful in Fu's hands. Fu laid the swords next to the soldier and got to work.

Fu removed the soldier's helmet, then his heavy, flexible armor. Fu was slipping off the man's boots when someone suddenly spoke behind him.

"What are you doing?"

Fu spun around and saw an average-size man. The man looked to be nearly thirty years old and had an extraordinarily long ponytail tied in a thick braid. He appeared to be wearing the uniform of the new Emperor, but Fu couldn't be sure in the smoky blackness. The soldier, however, saw that Fu was wearing an orange robe.

"Where have you been hiding, young monk?" the soldier asked in a calm, deep voice.

Fu responded by picking up the tiger hook swords.

"Put the weapons down, boy," the soldier said. "I have no interest in killing a child. I'll only take you prisoner. I'll ask you again, where were you hiding?"

Fu snarled and leaped at the soldier.

The soldier jumped backward gracefully and pulled a straight sword from a sheath slung at his side. Fu stopped and took notice. That jump was impressive, and only the most elite fighters carried a straight sword.

"Stand down, young monk," said the soldier as he draped his long braid forward over his shoulder and tucked it into his wide red sash. "You are no match for me."

Fu's mind began to race. Swordplay was his strong suit, but he knew nothing about this stranger's skill. And what he knew about the stranger's weapon worried him. While broadswords took one thousand hours to master, straight swords, like this soldier's, took more than ten thousand. The soldier had unsheathed it perfectly and held it in one hand instead of two—one hand to swing the long, rigid double-edged blade, and the other to counterbalance and fight. This man knew what he was doing.

Despite the night's coolness, Fu began to sweat. The tiger hooks he held were specifically designed to counter weapons like the straight sword, but he had never fought with Sing's pair. He had only fought with his own tiger hook swords, and every weapon had a spirit of its own. Fu put his faith in the spirits within Sing's hook swords and rushed forward.

The soldier took a defensive posture as Fu swung one hook sword high and one low, attempting to confuse his opponent—but the soldier expertly jumped over the low swing and blocked the high swing with his straight sword. On his way back to earth, the soldier let loose a terrific kick straight into Fu's exposed chest. Fu stumbled backward and groaned from the impact of the soldier's hard-soled boot. Fu was quite sure he had never been kicked that hard in his entire life.

A smile rose from the soldier's thin lips. "I will give you one more chance, monk. Lay down your weapons."

Fu took a deep breath and attacked again. This time, he slashed low with both swords. The soldier jumped high over Fu's sweeping weapons, but Fu twisted both wrists up powerfully and continued his swing toward the airborne soldier. The soldier swung his sword down to protect himself.

As the soldier's straight sword met the hook swords, Fu twisted both wrists outward and pulled his arms apart, locking the hooks around the soldier's straight blade. Fu dropped to the ground and rolled 360 degrees on his side, ripping the straight sword from the soldier's grasp. As Fu flipped up onto his feet, he arched his back and released the pressure on the hooks slightly. The soldier's sword sailed onto the roof of the burning bathhouse.

The soldier stood before Fu, weaponless. He smiled again and adjusted his long braid.

"I've never seen that particular maneuver, monk. Very dangerous for you, yet most effective."

"It's an original," Fu growled.

"Excellent. Though you appear to be very young, you're already quite skilled. I'm impressed. It's a good thing I've come prepared."

The soldier pulled a dagger from his sash and something fell to the ground. Fu realized that it was one of the dragon scrolls. The soldier saw the spark of recognition in Fu's eyes and nodded his head.

"If this document were not of the utmost importance, I might have considered giving it to you in exchange for an education in your unorthodox hook sword attacks. As it is, I cannot. My apologies."

When the soldier bent over to retrieve the scroll, Fu attacked for the third time. The soldier leaped back with the scroll in one hand, his dagger in the other. Fu took a basic swing with one hook sword to test the man's reaction with the short knife. The soldier leaped backward again, this time landing awkwardly on the helmet Fu had removed from the dead soldier.

Fu sprang forward, hitting his off-balance opponent square in the chest with a flying side kick. The soldier hit the ground flat on his back and Fu pounced, landing heavily on the man's chest. Fu's knees pinned the soldier's arms to the ground.

The soldier's dark eyes widened.

Fu swung both hook swords straight down in front of himself. The hooked ends of each blade dug deep into the earth on either side of the soldier's head, the hand-guard daggers stopping a hair's width above the soldier's throat. The soldier swallowed hard and his Adam's apple brushed against the very tip of one of the crescent-shaped daggers. A tiny stream of blood trickled down his neck.

The soldier looked Fu in the eye and said, "I admit defeat. Please, warrior monk—take the scrolls and leave me with my life. I will then owe you a life. On my honor, I will never forget the debt."

Fu growled and thought how easy it would be to lean down upon the handles and release the man's spirit. But taking a life was far more difficult than he had imagined. The soldier offered not only what Fu sought but also a favor for the future. It seemed Fu would gain more by letting this man live than by destroying him.

"Close your eyes!" Fu snarled.

The soldier did as he was told.

As soon as the man's eyelids met, Fu gripped both hook-sword handles with his left hand and released his right. He bent his right arm sharply and leaned forward, swinging his elbow across his body, over the crisscrossed swords. The point of his elbow struck the soldier in the left temple, knocking the man out cold.

Fu took a deep breath and stood. He leaned the handles of the hook swords onto the man's chest, leaving the crescent daggers dangerously close to the man's neck. Then he yanked the man's thick braid out of his sash and removed three dragon scrolls. Fu took the fourth scroll from the soldier's limp hand.

Fu concealed the scrolls securely within the folds of his own robe and looked down at Sing's tiger hook swords still lying over the soldier's throat. Those hook swords were fine weapons, but they were very difficult to transport. Fu decided to leave them in their current position to help remind the soldier of his promise.

His mission accomplished, Fu ran for the main gate—and into the worst surprise of the entire night.

CHAPTER 8

Fu stopped running just short of the main gate. Something didn't feel right. He stared through the smoky moonlight—up, down, forward, back, left, right.

Nothing.

Feeling like he had no time to waste, Fu took several steps backward, then shot forward. After six long strides, he was at top speed. On his seventh, he saw movement out of the corner of his eye. By then, it was too late.

Someone dove out from behind one of the gates and smashed headlong into him. Together they tumbled into the grass, and Fu managed to break loose of the fierce grip on his robe only by biting his opponent's arm. Fu sprang to his feet, and his opponent did the same. It was Ying.

Ying's carved face grimaced as he slipped his hand up one of his oversize sleeves and rubbed his arm.

"Where are you going in such a hurry, Pussycat?" he asked.

"As far away from you as possible," Fu replied, spitting out the words along with the horrible taste in his mouth.

Ying smiled. "Why spend your life running? Join me. I could use someone as feisty and fierce as you."

"Never."

Ying leaned forward and his black eyes sparkled. "Come on, Fu. Join me, and your rice bowl will always be overflowing. You'll never have to sweep another floor again, or wash somebody else's dirty socks. In my world, warriors are at the top of the food chain, not the bottom. What else are you going to do? Especially now that Grandmaster is gone."

Fu glared at Ying.

"That's right," Ying said. "Grandmaster is dead. I released his soul just a few moments ago."

Fu's eyes narrowed. "You're lying."

"Do you honestly think I would be standing here if he were still breathing?"

Fu shuddered like a cat thrown in an icy river. *Ying is probably telling the truth,* he thought. *Ying never left anything unfinished.*

Ying continued to rub his arm under his sleeve. "I'm not kidding, Fu. Grandmaster is dead. And it's a good thing, too. He wasn't the holy man everyone thought he was. I did you and everyone else a favor by killing him."

"Fu! Run!" someone shouted through the smoke. Fu looked up and saw Grandmaster limping toward them. He was dragging one leg, and one arm hung uselessly at his side.

"Stay back, you silver-tongued demon!" Ying shrieked at Grandmaster.

"Fu! Leap!" Grandmaster shouted.

Fu leaped backward as Ying suddenly whipped around and snapped his wrist outward in a blur. Fu saw a glint of metal and felt something brush against his right cheek. That side of his face immediately felt like it had caught fire. Blood poured across his jaw, down the side of his neck. It was Ying's chain whip! Fu remembered that Ying had designed the long, rigid, interlocking segments to be concealed in an oversize sleeve.

Fu turned in time to see Ying swing the metal whip at Grandmaster. Grandmaster dropped his head to avoid the sharp, weighted end, and Ying released the whip from his hand in mid-swing while thrusting his other hand straight out toward Grandmaster. There was a terrific *BOOM!* and Grandmaster stumbled backward as a hole opened in his chest. He slumped to the ground, dead.

Fu roared. Pain shot from the right corner of his mouth all the way up to his ear as the slice in his cheek opened wider.

Ying dropped the smoking *qiang* he had hidden up his sleeve and turned toward Fu. He bared his razor-sharp teeth and flicked out his forked tongue.

Above the crackling roar of the burning compound came a desperate cry.

"Major Ying! Come quickly! It concerns the scrolls!"

Ying turned his head toward the shouts, and Fu followed his gaze through the smoke. In the distance, the soldier Fu had fought with earlier—the one with the extraordinarily long ponytail—stood on the roof of the burning bathhouse.

The soldier called out to Ying again, and Fu took advantage of the distraction. He bolted through the open gate.

CHAPTER 9

Ying's number one soldier stood on the roof of the bathhouse, waiting for Ying. His name was Tonglong, which meant "praying mantis" in his native Cantonese dialect. Like the mantis, he was known for both his patience and speed. And like the mantis, he was sophisticated and complex. So was his fighting style.

Tonglong was twenty-nine years old and the undisputed second-in-command of Ying's troops. His long, thick ponytail stood out among men. By the time Ying reached the bathhouse, nearly one hundred and fifty soldiers stood in a dark, smoke-filled court-yard, staring up at Tonglong.

"What is going on here?" Ying demanded as the crowd parted before him.

Tonglong bent over to lift his sword off the red roof tiles. Shrouded in flickering flames, he looked down at Ying.

"A young monk has taken possession of the scrolls," Tonglong said calmly, adjusting his long braid forward over his shoulder.

"What?" Ying shouted. "Say that again!"

"A young monk has taken possession of the scrolls, sir. I am sorry. I am completely at fault."

"How could you be so incompetent?" Ying asked, staring up at Tonglong. "What happened?"

"I retrieved the scrolls from the library as you ordered," Tonglong said, ignoring the flames around him. "But then I encountered a rather stout young monk. He attacked me with a pair of tiger hook swords and tricked me with a very cunning maneuver. He managed to hurl my sword onto this rooftop and knock me unconscious. I suppose that is when he took the scrolls from my sash. I climbed up here to retrieve my sword and saw you in the distance. I hope I didn't interrupt anything important."

Ying scanned the ground and spotted Sing's tiger hook swords. He grabbed them and waved them high over his head.

"Are these the hook swords the young monk used?"

"Yes," Tonglong replied. "The very same."

Ying snarled and ran straight at the outer wall of the bathhouse. His body remained perpendicular to the ground as he made two long strides right up the side of the brick building, his legs working like he was climbing a set of stairs. Warrior monks usually completed this maneuver by executing a backflip. Not Ying. The balls of his bare feet and his long toenails pushed off subtle irregularities in the brick, and he shot straight into the air. He stretched both arms up as high as he could with a hook sword extended in each hand and caught the outermost edge of the roof's lip with both hooks. Then he swung himself up onto the roof, taking the hook swords with him. He approached Tonglong atop the burning building, his leathery feet treading lightly on the hot roof tiles.

"Fool!" Ying screamed in Tonglong's face, spit flying off his forked tongue. "*You hope you didn't interrupt anything?* What's wrong with you? I had that same fat little monk in my grasp, and I let him go! Why? So that I could come over here and help *you*! I would have had the boy *and* the scrolls if not for you! ARRRRRGH!"

Ying lunged furiously at Tonglong, whirling both hook swords. Tonglong expertly avoided Ying's attack by dodging and weaving and scrambling up and down the slick curved tiles covering the steep pitch. Flames leaped skyward through growing holes in the roof, and Tonglong used the flames to his advantage. By using them as a shield, he managed to keep space between himself and the hook swords. He did not counterattack.

Ying stopped his assault for a moment, and Tonglong slid down to the very edge of the roof, directly in front of the soldiers. A flickering wall of flame separated him and Ying as he kneeled down on the blistering hot tiles. The tip of his long braid brushed the rooftop.

"Sir, I ask your forgiveness," Tonglong said.

Breathing heavily, Ying let the hook swords drop to his sides. He shifted his weight from foot to foot to keep his bare feet from burning.

Tonglong lowered his eyes. "I am truly sorry, sir. The boy was incredibly skilled. Had I known he was no ordinary young monk, I would have reacted differently. My guard was down because—"

"Don't EVER let your guard down!" Ying shouted, raising the hook swords once more. "Not on my command!"

"I will never make this same mistake again, sir!" Tonglong said, looking up. "Please forgive my incompetence."

"ARRRRRGH!"

Ying threw the tiger hook swords far across the compound and leaped down from the high roof in a perfectly executed double flip.

"Everyone, follow me!" Ying shouted. "Now!"

Tonglong waited for Ying and the others to travel some distance before he tucked his thick braid into his sash and leaped down in a perfect triple flip.

Ying led the group to the main gate and instructed them to form a circle around Grandmaster's limp body. He strode to the center of the moonlit ring of soldiers.

"Men, we set out to destroy Cangzhen Temple and all its monks," Ying announced. "I am afraid we have only partially succeeded. At least one young monk has escaped, and there may be more. A group of you will collect every dead monk, and I will personally review each and every body. Another group will count all our fallen soldiers. I fear we have lost more than two thousand men to just one hundred monks. This is inexcusable, and my response will be additional intensive training for those of you who are still breathing. I refuse to continue with such incompetence."

The soldiers cast their eyes to the ground and shuffled their feet.

"Look at me when I'm talking!" Ying commanded. "All of you!"

The men looked up at Ying's contorted, raging face.

"Tonglong, bring me your sword!"

Tonglong hesitated.

"Prove your loyalty to me, Tonglong," Ying said. "Trust that I will do what is best for the group and for the Emperor. Bring me your sword."

Tonglong hesitated for another moment, then slipped his sheathed sword from his sash. He formally handed the heirloom over, bowing low. Ying ripped the scabbard from the sword and cast it disrespectfully aside onto the dusty ground. He raised the sword high over his head with both hands.

In one long, sweeping motion, Ying brought the sword down in a powerful arc. The sword breezed over Tonglong's bowed head as Ying twisted around. When the arc was complete, the sword dug deep into the earth, and Grandmaster's head rolled away from his lifeless body.

Ying released the sword from the ground with a rough jerk and cast it aside irreverently. Then he grabbed Grandmaster's bald head by one ear and threw it at Tonglong. Tonglong caught the spinning object with outstretched arms, ignoring the blood that pelted him from head to toe. Tonglong respectfully placed his catch on the ground beside him and wiped his bloody hands across the front of his green silk robe.

"I promised to take that to the Emperor," Ying said to Tonglong. "You will take it to him for me at once. You will also give him the unfortunate news that my mission is not yet complete, and I would not dream of accepting the title of General until I have fulfilled my end of our agreement. Understood?"

"Completely, sir," Tonglong said.

"Good."

Ying turned to his number-two-in-command, Commander Woo. The powerful, stocky man stood at attention. He adjusted his armor.

"Commander Woo, you and half the men will remain here to sort and count bodies. Then you will strip the armor from our fallen comrades. You will work through the night."

"Yes, sir!" Commander Woo replied.

Ying turned to Captain Yue, his number-three-in-command. Captain Yue sighed and fidgeted with his large silk hat.

"Captain Yue!" Ying said. "Pay attention! You will break the remaining men into groups and spread out to inform every village within one hundred *li* that I am searching for anyone resembling a young monk. Five monks between the ages of eleven and thirteen may be out there, and one of them has a set of scrolls that I want back. You are to inform one and all that it will mean instant death for them, their entire family, and all their neighbors if they are found to be harboring one or more of these monks or the scrolls. Anyone coming in contact with one of these monks or the scrolls is to notify me without delay. Tell everyone along the way the name and location of this 'secret' temple, as I will be waiting here for updates. Is that clear?"

Captain Yue nodded and plucked at his spotless silk robe. Ying scowled and leaned forward, slowly turning within the circle of soldiers. His black eyes connected with every man in the group.

"Keep in mind that those of you who remain here will have no easy task," Ying said, "for you must keep your eyes and ears open whether asleep or awake. I am confident at least one sentimental young monk will return. Now form your groups and get moving! You can find me here at this wretched place until further notice."

ƒu raced on. The earth felt the pounding of his feet as he leaped over boulders and darted between enormous, ancient trees. His eyes fed off the occasional moonbeam with feline proficiency, his bare feet cunningly avoiding the numerous snarled roots hiding in the deep shadows. Fu's heart pounded, forcing bursts of hot, sticky blood out of the slice in his cheek. He kept his head tilted to one side so that the blood would run down his neck and onto the collar of his robe instead of dripping onto the ground, leaving a telltale trail for Ying and his men to follow.

All alone, Fu's mind raced even faster than his feet. *How could Ying do this?*

Fu often grew angry over things that happened to

him at Cangzhen. But he would never have retaliated by killing someone. That was crazy. He had never even dreamed of killing Ying, who had picked on him constantly. One of Fu's older brothers once suggested killing Ying as retaliation for Ying's publicly blaming the death of his only friend on Grandmaster—but the older brother was just joking. Everyone knew Ying's comments were made out of sadness and denial. Many of the monks even felt sorry for Ying because they were certain that if anyone was to blame for the death, it was Ying himself. So instead of punishing Ying for his comments, the senior monks had been satisfied when Ying announced he was leaving the temple forever to wander the surrounding forests. They knew how painfully alone he would be, and they agreed that perpetual loneliness was punishment enough for his actions.

64

Fu originally disagreed and thought that Ying should receive at least forty whacks with a bamboo rod. However, now that he was running solo into the unknown himself, Fu was beginning to think perhaps the monks had been right. Perhaps loneliness hit harder than bamboo.

Fu began to ache deep down. He realized that he had never really been alone before. He had always worked, practiced, studied, ate, and even slept with at least one of his four brothers around. He used to complain about never being alone, and Grandmaster had always told him that you should be careful about what you wish for. Fu began to think no truer words had ever been spoken. His brothers could be annoying, but at least he had always had someone to argue with.

Fu did realize that he and his brothers occasionally got along. One thing they had in common was their negative feelings about their daily schedules. They all followed the rigid plans Grandmaster laid out for them hour by hour, and they were never given any free time. Fu had felt the strongest about wanting time alone, which is why he was surprised to discover that now that he seemed to have all the time in the world, he wasn't sure what he should do with it.

Fu's mind continued to race further and further away from the task at hand—which was to run as fast as possible through the dark forest without getting injured—until a thick tree root reached up and grabbed his foot. He went down hard.

Fu lay on a bed of dead leaves, catching his breath. He scolded himself for thinking too much and lifted his head as a salty drop of water fell from his right eye, sinking deep into the slice across his cheek. He successfully fought off the urge to cry out and squeezed both eyes shut, cutting off the flow of liquid. Then he stood. None of his bones seemed to be broken, and none of his joints felt twisted. He stuck his right foot into a small pool of moonlight and saw that the top was beginning to bruise. His foot hurt a lot, but not as much as his cheek, which hurt only half as much as the pain growing deep inside his heart.

The wind picked up for a moment, and Fu noticed that the night seemed chillier. It must be the altitude.

He had intentionally run toward the closest low-lying mountain, knowing that if he traveled high enough he should be able to find something that would help keep his bad situation from getting worse: bloodmoss.

Like self-defense, herbal medicine was a matter of survival, so it was studied by all warrior monks. Fu ran his index finger across the slice in his cheek. Facial cuts always bled profusely, and his was exceptionally long and deep. If he lost too much blood, he would pass out, and who knew what might happen to him then? Bloodmoss would stop the bleeding. It didn't work for everyone—not even any of his brothers—but it worked wonders for him. It would be difficult to find in the dark, but he couldn't wait for the sun to rise. Fu noticed more moonlight striking the ground in the distance, which meant the canopy was beginning to thin. That was a good sign. He started walking.

Soon Fu found what he was looking for—a clump of bloodmoss poking out from under a fallen log. Once he had a fistful, he located a smooth, palm-size rock to use as a pounding tool, and a large flat rock to serve as a makeshift tabletop. After brushing most of the dirt and bits of rotten log off the moss, Fu began to pound it to a pulp. He worked quickly, making as little noise as possible. Things weren't coming together quite the way he expected until he remembered that he was missing one key ingredient: water. To get the appropriate paste-like consistency necessary to plug a wound, you needed to add a little bit of liquid. Fu had to improvise. He spit on the pulverized mass.

After a little more pounding and mashing, Fu scooped up the paste with one hand and applied it with the other. Almost immediately, the blood stopped flowing. The sharp stinging sensation he felt from the breeze blowing into the wound also stopped. However, the wind managed to irritate him in other ways. It chilled his robes, which were still wet from lying in the barrel, and blew the fabric up against his body, where it clung tightly. Fu shivered. He needed shelter. Fortunately, one thing the mountainous forest did not lack was rocks. Rocks of all sizes. He located an outcropping with an opening opposite the wind and curled up inside.

Fu could not recall ever feeling so drained. His training at Cangzhen had been tough, but he had never pushed this hard for this long and never before had so much adrenaline pumped through his system. Fu gave in to his exhaustion. But even as his body relaxed and his breathing slowed, his mind continued to race.

Where are my brothers? he wondered. *Why didn't they stay and try to do something? And now that they are gone and I'm alone with the scrolls, what should I do with them?*

Fu was perplexed. He was driven by instinct, not reason. It was not his nature to think so much.

Exhausted, cold, and alone, he closed his eyes.

CHAPTER

11

"How much longer do you think he'll be down there?" the soldier asked.

"I have no idea," Commander Woo replied. "It's only been a few hours, but as far as I'm concerned, Major Ying can stay down there forever."

"What do you think he's doing?"

"I don't even want to know. Just stop your yapping and keep digging. If he sees us before we're finished, he may finish *us*. I never asked permission to do this."

Ying lay asleep on the cool earth inside the Cangzhen escape tunnel, oblivious to what his men were doing above ground. Soon after he'd inspected the dead monks and confirmed that Fu and the other four boys had escaped, he'd gone below ground. Ying was solitary by nature and often needed time alone.

Alone time was very important to Ying when he lived at Cangzhen, too—and he used to steal some whenever he had the chance. For years, the escape tunnel had been his preferred hideout. It was a place where he could be by himself. A place where he could be himself. Though the world saw him as an eagle, in his heart he knew he was an all-powerful dragon. Over the years, the tunnel had become Ying's own private lair. No one else ever bothered to go down there because of the concealed traps. No one, that is, except Fu.

Occasionally, Ying would drift off to sleep in the tunnel. When he failed to show up for a meal or training session, someone would have to go down there and wake him. Ying hated to be woken and would lash out immediately at whoever disturbed him. So none of the monks liked to go near him when he slept. None of the monks, that is, except Fu, who seemed to derive a special pleasure from irritating Ying. Fu would eagerly volunteer every time Ying needed to be woken, especially down in the dark tunnel, where no one was watching. Fu would use his eerily efficient low-light vision to stalk Ying slowly— silently—before waking him with a powerful punch or kick.

And so a special relationship had formed between Ying and Fu. Ying would torment Fu during the day, and Fu would strike back while Ying slept. Ying's feelings toward Fu were a big part of the reason he needed to have some alone time right now. He was upset that the scrolls had been taken, but he was especially upset that Fu had been the one to do it. As he lay there, Ying dreamed he was out on the trail, searching for Fu. Ying loved the thrill of the hunt, and it pained him that he could hunt no more. It was now his responsibility to direct the efforts of others. All he could do was sit back and watch.

Ying felt something brush against his nose and woke instantly, lashing out. But there was no one there. Small rocks and bits of dirt were raining down on his head, a steady stream that quickly turned into a rushing river. Ying managed to roll off to one side and curl into a ball as the river became a tidal wave of debris, and the sky opened above him.

Commander Woo leaned his squat, powerful body over and stared down into the huge hole. The soldier who had been helping him dig lay on the floor of the escape tunnel, atop a mound of earth. The soldier pushed aside his broken shovel and stared up at Commander Woo framed in the early-morning light.

"Are you all right down there?" Commander Woo asked the soldier.

"Yeah, yeah," the man replied, groaning. "I *told* you we shouldn't have dug in this spot! I had a feeling the tunnel was—"

"Shhh!" Commander Woo urged in a harsh whisper. "Not so loud! Major Ying is probably still down there somewhere. I don't want him to hear us."

"Relax," the soldier said. "If Major Ying was—"

A section of the mound next to the soldier's head suddenly exploded, giving way to a perfectly formed eagle-claw fist. The fist clamped down on the man's throat. Four long fingernails sank deep along one side of his larynx. A razor-sharp thumbnail sank in on the opposite side. The fist squeezed until sound no longer came from the soldier's mouth. Then the claw abruptly released. The soldier scrambled off the mound, trying desperately to cry out for help. He was unsuccessful.

The entire mound shifted, and Major Ying rose from the rubble like a dirty phoenix. He leaped onto the highest point of the mound, then leaped again and soared up through the hole, his arms spread wide. He landed in front of Commander Woo, who took several steps back.

"What do you think you are doing?" Ying asked, shaking his head violently. Dirt flew in every direction.

Commander Woo cleared his throat. "Digging a hole, sir."

"I can see that, you imbecile. *Why* are you digging?"

"We need to bury the dead, sir."

"Bury the dead?" Ying said, leaning toward Commander Woo.

"Yes, sir," Commander Woo replied. "We should bury our fallen soldiers. We should bury the monks, too. We need to respect the dead."

"And when do you think you will have time for this?" Ying asked.

"We have already begun, sir."

"I can see that! It will take you and the men days to dig enough holes."

"We know, sir," Commander Woo said hesitantly. "But the men think it's worth it. They are willing to put in the extra effort required. They are afraid."

Ying scowled and the creases in his face deepened. "Afraid of what?"

"We discovered something earlier. Something very disturbing."

"Like what?" Ying asked.

"One of the bodies is missing," Commander Woo said nervously. "One of the fallen monks. Actually, not just any monk—the Cangzhen Grandmaster."

"WHAT?" Ying shouted.

"I know, sir," Commander Woo replied. "It is hard to believe, but it's true. The men believe the body went in search of its head."

"That's ridiculous," Ying scoffed. "Headless corpses don't just get up and walk away."

"That's exactly what I told the men! If you ask me, I think some other ghosts came along and took it."

"WHAT?" Ying shouted again. "Have you lost your mind?"

"Sir, there is no other possible explanation," Commander Woo said. "We have had at least two sentries at every gate since before you went down into the tunnel. Tonglong positioned the sentries himself before he left. No living creature could have possibly gotten in and then back out again without us noticing. It had to be spirits. Without a proper burial, the souls of *all* these men will become hungry ghosts here in our world instead of moving on to the next life. We must be respectful. Who knows what they might do?"

Ying shoved Commander Woo to the ground and stepped over him, straddling Woo's thick, stumpy body. Commander Woo normally feared no man, but he slammed his eyes closed when he saw Ying curl back his lips and stick out his forked tongue.

"Listen to me," Ying hissed. "The men should fear *me* far more than any ghost. Tell them to stop digging immediately. They will ALL spend their time stripping the armor off the dead soldiers like I ordered. Then you and the men will build carts to transport it. It will take you a very long time to complete this task. You will bury no one."

"But—"

"But what?" Ying said.

"There is something else, sir," Commander Woo said, his eyes wide. "The men are convinced they are being watched. That is all they keep talking about. I believe them, too. I feel it myself. The men think that some of the dead have already become hungry ghosts, and that they are watching—waiting for us to go to sleep so that they can devour our souls."

"Then tell the men to stay awake!" Ying shouted. "NOW GET TO WORK!"

Ying turned away, shaking his head. *Superstitious fools,* he thought. For a moment, Ying considered telling Commander Woo that he was right to believe something was watching because he felt it, too—and he was pretty sure he knew what it was. In the end, however, Ying decided against it. He didn't want his men to be any more distracted than they already were.

Fu tossed and turned on the chilly, damp ground, stuck somewhere between awake and asleep. Each time his mind sank below the waves of consciousness, the same three questions would arise and his brain would bob back to the surface.

Why did Ying do this?

Where are my brothers?

What should be done with the scrolls?

The questions were relentless. Nothing in his previous training had prepared him for this. He had always relied on instinct, reacting to outside forces. Never before had he battled forces within himself. And never before had he been in a position to choose his own path. Even though he hated it, a course had always been laid before him by Grandmaster. But Grandmaster was gone. Fu would have to forge a path of his own.

"Always remember, you represent Cangzhen." That's what Grandmaster had said back at the temple during the attack. Fu knew that *Cangzhen* meant "hidden truth" and that Cangzhen's founders had once been wanderers like he was now. Wherever the founders traveled, they had been the defenders of Truth and the deliverers of Justice. Fu realized that he was obligated to do the same.

But where should I go? Fu wondered. *What should I do next?*

Fu pleaded to his ancestors for some kind of sign, and as his mind sank into the depths of unconsciousness one more time, he thought he heard an answer.

Somewhere in the distance, a tiger screamed and men cheered. Fu awoke instantly, springing to his feet, his large, bald head narrowly missing the low rock outcropping that had sheltered him while he struggled with sleep. Someone was torturing a tiger. He could hear it. He could feel it. And he wasn't about to stand for it. After all, he was a Cangzhen warrior monk. It was his duty to defend Truth and deliver Justice. With the sun just beginning to show itself above the treetops to the east, Fu checked to make sure the scrolls were secure in the folds of his robe and raced down the rocky mountain slope back into the heavy forest.

Fu was well aware that knowing your enemy is

often the key to victory. As he ran, he struggled to remember what little he knew about tiger hunters. Hunters—if they could be called that—would dig a large pit in the middle of a tiger trail, line it with sharp bamboo stakes secured deep in the ground, and cover the pit loosely with brush. Then they would set up a "drive." Armed with long spears, the hunters would walk in a group along a tiger trail, making a tremendous commotion. Tigers preferred to steer clear of people, so the tiger being hunted would run ahead of the group in an effort to stay out of the way, usually sticking to the path it routinely followed. If it wasn't careful, it would fall into the pit, landing on the spikes, impaled and stuck at the bottom with little or no mobility. The hunters would come running—but not to end the animal's suffering. Instead, they would slash the tiger repeatedly with the razor-sharp metal tips of their long spears, tormenting the tiger for hours until it slowly bled to death.

Men did this simply to make themselves feel powerful. They called themselves "sport" hunters. Fu was not about to let any man make himself feel powerful at the expense of an animal. Especially a tiger.

Before long, Fu was close enough that he could hear men talking. He slowed down. There seemed to be three men and a boy—one of the voices was quite small. Two of the voices were so loud and brash, Fu thought half of China could hear their boasting. Those two were certainly hunters.

"How strong you are, good sir, standing before the beast's offspring so calmly," the first hunter said.

"And how brave your son is at your side, wielding his spear," said the second hunter.

Fu grew enraged. *Bravery? Strength?* These men had dug a hole and tricked a tiger. What did they know about bravery and strength? Fu's eyes narrowed. His nostrils flared. He would teach these braggarts something about bravery and strength.

Just then, something whimpered. Softly once, then louder a second time.

"Stick him again, brave boy!" the second hunter shouted.

"No, no!" the first hunter said excitedly. "Don't *stick* him, *finish* him! Finish the little monster while I finish his mother in the pit!"

There was a short grunt from the person with the small voice, and then another whimper—followed by a huge roar. So there were *two* tigers! A mother in a pit and her cub off to one side. Fu rushed toward the voices, scanning the ground as he ran. Without breaking stride, he reached down and grabbed a fallen tree limb about as long as he was tall. He snapped several small twigs off the old, dried-out branch, throwing them to the ground. What was left in his hands was a makeshift staff that was so old and dry it would most likely shatter upon its first impact. But all he needed was one shot. Fu lowered his head and bounded through a line of tall, dew-drenched ferns.

When he burst out the other side, he was running at top speed.

Taken completely by surprise, the hunters saw a large, robust, orange-robed boy racing toward them carrying a long, crooked stick. His head was bald, and large beads of dew clung to it, glistening in the early-morning light. The collar of his robe was streaked with crusted, dried blood on one side, and his cheek on that side seemed to have a patch of moss growing out of it. Fire burned in his eyes as he headed first one way, then changed direction slightly and went straight for the hunter standing closest to the pit.

Sometimes a slight change of direction can make all the difference—for better or for worse. When Fu first burst into the clearing, he saw a large tiger cub off to the right, cornered against a wall of rock by a Gentleman clad head to toe in shimmering green silk. A small, similarly dressed boy about Fu's age stood next to the man, holding a decorated spear. The boy timidly poked at the cub while the man stood stern and silent, his arms folded across the front of his elegant robe. Fu was on his way to stop the boy when he saw two hunters standing over a large pit. One of them was poised to launch a spear with both hands. Fu recognized that position. That was a final thrust stance. That hunter was about to finish the mother tiger. Fu changed directions in mid-stride.

Uncertain of whether he should act or react against his oncoming attacker, the hunter with the raised spear hesitated as Fu approached. Fu recognized the man's hesitation and threw himself to the ground. Fu rolled forward hard and fast over his right shoulder, then popped up onto his feet and lunged forward, powerfully thrusting one end of his stick straight out with both hands. Fu anticipated significant resistance when the end of the stick met the hunter's midsection, sending the man flying backward into the pit. One cannot even begin to imagine Fu's surprise when the stick met no resistance whatsoever.

The second hunter had managed to knock Fu's target out of the way the very moment Fu started his roll. With nothing there to receive the energy from his mighty thrust, Fu's unchecked momentum carried him directly into the pit.

CHAPTER 13

The mother tiger lay on her side at the bottom of the pit, a long bamboo stake sticking straight up from the ground through one of her hindquarters. A second stake protruded from her abdomen, standing firm as the skin of her belly rode up and down its shaft every time she shifted positions or took a deep breath. Embedded in her shoulder was the broken shaft of a decorated spear.

Without warning, a large man-child suddenly sailed into the pit headfirst with his arms out before him. The tiger roared in anger and twisted her head up and back, eager to latch onto something with her ferocious jaws. When she felt the man-child's sleeve brush against her muzzle, she clamped down with all her might. There was a tremendous crunch, and the man-child twisted in midair. His arm came loose from his body, shattering into a thousand pieces. Two heavy, bare feet stomped down hard on her rib cage, and the man-child sprang back up into the air, pushing off the side of her chest. The man-child never uttered a sound. That was strange. He was nearly halfway to the upper edge of the pit before she realized why. She had not ripped a limb from his body. She had shattered some kind of tree limb. She roared as she lifted her entire body up as best she could and slashed out at the retreating man-child with one of her monstrous claws. This time, the man-child yelped in pain.

Fu landed on the far edge of the pit, toad-style. He hopped forward twice in an effort to get some space between him and the pit, his backside stinging with each thrust of his legs. He stood and turned to inspect the damage. The very tip of one of the tiger's dagger-like nails had ripped a gaping hole in the back of both his robe and his pants, and skimmed along the surface of his skin. He didn't seem to be bleeding, but it was hard to tell—he couldn't see around himself. As he stretched and turned in every direction trying to complete his inspection, he realized that the hunters on the other side of the pit were roaring with laughter. Fu glared at them.

"Iron Toad Escapes the Claw of Death by the Seat

of His Pants!" the first hunter laughed. "What a great story!"

"I am no toad," Fu growled. "I am a tiger."

"Sure you are, kid," the first hunter replied. "Look, that was pretty amazing what you just did. So out of respect for your skill—and your amazing luck—I'm going to forget that you nearly killed me. Okay? Here, let me give you some of the antiseptic herbs I brought along . . . BUTT—you're going to have to apply them yourself!"

The first hunter howled with laughter. The second hunter howled along with him.

"I need nothing from your kind!" Fu spat.

Both hunters stopped laughing.

"Excuse me?" the first hunter said. "*Our kind*, you say? And just what kind would that be?"

"Cowardly peasants with no respect for life!"

The first hunter raised an eyebrow. "Look, little man," he said, "I just offered to help you after you attacked me for no apparent reason. If you keep this up, you're—"

"Enough!" Fu roared.

The hunters looked at one another, disbelief on their faces. The first hunter slammed the blunt end of his spear into the ground and began to walk around the pit toward Fu. Seeing this, the Gentleman spoke from behind the hunters.

"STOP! Do not take another step. Please."

The first hunter stopped, and the Gentleman

turned to his son beside him. "Do not let this cub get away. Understand?"

The boy nodded his head quietly, and the Gentleman turned toward Fu.

"Excuse me, young man. Just who do you think you are, talking to these men that way? You should treat your elders with respect."

"I have no respect for their kind," Fu sneered. "Or for yours. In fact, I am certain I have even less respect for you."

"Why do you say such things?" the Gentleman asked.

"Why? Because you're planning to kill these tigers! That's why! And because you're pushing your son to do something that he doesn't want to do. What has that cub ever done to him? Or to you? Or to anyone else?"

"It's not what the cub has done," the Gentleman replied. "It's what he might do."

"What he *might* do?" Fu said. "That's crazy!"

"You do not understand, young man. If you would just—"

Fu had heard enough. He roared and ran straight toward the pit, leaping high into the air when he reached the edge. He landed with plenty of room to spare on the other side of the pit and spun around to face his closest opponent—the second hunter. The man stood several paces away, armed with a spear.

Out of the corner of his eye, Fu saw that the first hunter had run around to the opposite side of the pit.

The man stepped up to the edge, grasped his spear with both hands, and raised it up as he had done earlier. The tiger growled again and lifted its head, baring its teeth.

"What are you doing?" Fu cried.

"Mind your own business, monk," the first hunter said. "This hunt doesn't concern you."

"I'm making it my business!" Fu said.

"Then you will be sorry," the man replied, and thrust his spear into the tiger's thick neck. The tiger roared no more.

Something inside Fu's head snapped. The world went black before his eyes, and his ears closed themselves off to everything around him. For the rest of his life, Fu would never remember everything that happened next. For the rest of their lives, the others would never forget.

Fu attacked with lightning speed. He lunged at the second hunter so fast, the man only had time to push his spear out before him with both hands held wide, the spear parallel to the ground. It was a pitiful attempt at a defensive maneuver. Fu bent his elbows and drew both hands in to his chest with his wrists flexed up and back. He spread his fingers wide and curled them down and in, like tiger's claws, then exhaled powerfully as he thrust both hands forward, side by side. Fu's palms met the center point of the spear's shaft at full force and the shaft broke in two. His clawlike hands continued forward, clamping down powerfully on the hunter's throat as his weight and momentum sent them both tumbling to the ground. Fu released his right hand—his most powerful hand—and formed a fist. He smashed it into the side of his opponent's head, knocking the man out cold. Fu looked over at the first hunter.

The first hunter yanked his spear out of the tiger, its metal tip dripping blood, and ran around the pit toward Fu. Fu sprang to his feet, picked up one half of the second hunter's broken spear in each hand, and raced forward to meet his next opponent head on.

Three paces from Fu, the first hunter leaped high into the air. That was a mistake. Fu retained a balanced, level plane, bent his elbows back and up beyond his ears, then swung both halves of the wooden spear straight up into the first hunter's groin.

The man's eyes bulged and he cried out, pulling his knees up while still in midair. He landed in a heap on his side, immobilized. Fu was about to continue his assault on the man when he heard the Gentleman speak.

"It's okay, Son," the Gentleman said. "I understand your reservations. Turn away, if you wish."

The boy turned away from his father, and his eyes locked on Fu's. Staring coldly at the boy, Fu dropped the spear halves and picked up the whole, blood-stained spear that the first hunter had let fall to his side as he hit the ground. The boy cried out.

"Father!"

Fu quickly covered the distance between where he was and where he wanted to be. He swung the blunt end of the spear as hard as he could with both hands, into the boy's left ear. The boy fell to his knees, and his head slumped down. Blood began to trickle out of his ear. Seeing his son go down, the Gentleman lost all composure.

"Be gone, evil monk!" the Gentleman shouted. "I hope you've made yourself feel powerful, attacking an unarmed child!"

The man's words brought Fu back to his senses. In a daze, he watched as the tiger cub ran off.

"Look!" the Gentleman said. "You've accomplished your mission! The cub is free! Now leave me to tend to my son."

Fu didn't know what to say.

"I'm putting down my weapon," the Gentleman said as he laid down the decorated spear that he had taken from the boy. "Please, leave us be. I do not know where you learned such brutality, but where I come from, we care for one another. We do not beat one another. Now I wish to care for my son. Will you let me?"

The Gentleman's voice was strong, but his eyes were weak. Unsure of what he should say or do next, Fu resorted to doing what he always did when he was filled with uncertainty. He walked away.

CHAPTER 14

Fu leaned over a pool of clear spring water, tilting his head to one side until he saw his reflection. He looked as horrible as he felt. He lowered both hands into the cool water and rubbed them together, scraping off as much dried blood and dirt as possible. Then he scooped up a double handful of clean water to quench his thirst. His throat was painfully dry, and Fu realized as he drank that he hadn't had a single sip of fluid since early the night before, yet he had exerted himself more than ever before. He felt light-headed, and that feeling had been with him for some time. That must be the reason he could only remember bits and pieces of what happened earlier with the hunters. He seemed to recall that the hunters deserved everything they got—and then some—but Fu wasn't so sure about the boy. After all, the boy had done nothing to either him or the tiger in the pit, and the boy only poked the cub a couple times after the adults pressured him. As a Cangzhen warrior monk, it was his duty to dispense Justice—but he must take great care to dispense the right *amount* of Justice. Too much would make him and all Cangzhen monks look bad. The boy's father seemed to think he had gone too far. Perhaps he had.

Fu lowered his hands into the water again and watched as ripples radiated out far and wide across the pool's surface. What had he done? More importantly, what was he going to do next?

Too tired to think, Fu took another long drink and inspected the slice in his cheek. It felt like most of the bloodmoss had fallen out, and a quick check of his reflection verified that. What little moss remained was stuck securely inside the wound, intermixed with dried blood. It didn't look infected, but you could never be sure with bloodmoss. There was only one way to find out. Fu reached down into the pool and scooped up a single handful of cool, clean water. He rested his wounded cheek in his wet hand to soften the congealed mass, and after a few moments it appeared sufficiently soft. He hated this part. Fu picked at a corner of the wound until a small flap of bloodmoss and scab came loose, then he ripped the mass out in one continuous motion. Fu shuddered, his eyes watering for a moment.

Fu checked his reflection again. The slice in his cheek bled slightly, but it was clean blood. It wasn't infected, and it looked like it would scab over again soon enough. It also looked like it was going to leave a nasty scar. The image of Ying's hideously scarred face suddenly popped into his mind. He knew how much his own cheek hurt, and he couldn't imagine what Ying had endured—intentionally, no less. *What a fool,* Fu thought.

It was at that very moment Fu's heart skipped a beat. Where were the scrolls?

Fu quickly checked the folds of his robe, which had loosened during the fighting. To his relief, all four scrolls were still there. Wiping the newly formed sweat from his brow, he stood, feeling a stinging sensation on his backside. He had just made sure that his face wasn't infected, but perhaps his other cheeks were. His butt really hurt. Tigers were notorious for having rotten flesh embedded in the undersides of their claws, and anything they scratched was highly susceptible to infection. Fu struggled as he had earlier to see around himself in order to assess the damage. Finally, he decided to use the reflective properties of the water to aid him. He waded out into the pool a little ways and squatted, trying to get a better look. In the midst of his efforts, he heard a rustling in the undergrowth near one edge of the pool. Taken by surprise, Fu slipped on a moss-covered stone and splashed down in the pool.

In an effort to remain as inconspicuous as possible,

Fu rolled over onto his stomach and lay motionless with only his bald head visible above the waterline. A slight movement in the brush caught his eye. He strained to make out exactly who was spying on him. It turned out to be the tiger cub.

"What are you looking at?" Fu called out angrily as he stood, certain that he would scare the cub off. Instead, the cub cocked its head inquisitively to one side, listening.

"Look what you've made me do! My clothes didn't even have a chance to dry out from lying in that stupid barrel last night, and now the scrolls are soaked, too!"

The cub tilted its head the other way.

"I save your life, and this is how you thank me?"

The cub stepped a little closer to the pool, and Fu noticed for the first time two large blotches of bright red on one of the cub's sides. Both spots were definitely blood, and they looked bad. The wounds from the spear must be deep. The cub was still bleeding. It took another step toward the pool, wobbling slightly, and lowered its head to drink.

Watching the cub slowly lap up the water, Fu wondered what it ate. He hadn't eaten since supper the night before, and he had worked up a ferocious appetite. Now that he had quenched his thirst, he needed to find some food. Perhaps the hunters had had a camp, and maybe they had left some food there. Fu decided to take a look.

After a little more bending and twisting, Fu felt

confident that the long scratch from the mother tiger was not infected. He stuck his backside down into the cool water and wiggled around to flush out the wound—just in case—then sloshed back onto dry land.

Fu shivered. It was the season of Plum Blossoms, and the air was chilly. At least the days and nights would be growing warmer. If it were the season of Falling Plums, he would have nothing but colder days and very cold nights to look forward to. Fu nodded to the cub and headed back toward the clearing where he had encountered the hunters. For some reason the cub followed on its unsteady legs. Curious, Fu called to it several times, but the cub wouldn't get close to him. In fact, it lagged farther and farther behind with each step. Fu soon gave up.

Fu made it back to the large clearing, and the cub was nowhere in sight. It must have moved on alone. Or perhaps it just didn't want to go near its dead mother in the pit. Fu decided to steer clear of the pit, too. He already had enough bad memories.

While crisscrossing the clearing, Fu found the bag of antiseptic herbs the first hunter had mentioned. It must have fallen to the ground during their fight. He picked it up. He made a couple more passes across the clearing but found nothing more.

Fu decided to try and locate the hunters' camp next. As he looked for tracks left by the hunters on the hard ground, he thought he heard something. No, actually it was more like he felt something. It felt like someone was calling him. Fu looked around, but there was no one there. Still, the feeling grew stronger and stronger. He had never felt anything quite like it. He closed his eyes, trying to make sense of it. An image of the tiger cub suddenly popped into his mind. A memory. The tiger cub stood on wobbly legs next to the pool, then it followed him unsteadily for a short while until Fu finally lost sight of it. Had something happened to the cub? Fu decided to go back and take a look.

Fu only had to backtrack a little ways before he found the cub collapsed on the forest floor. It was panting heavily, its eyes rolled back in its head. Fu approached cautiously, but it became obvious almost immediately that caution wasn't necessary. The cub didn't seem to notice he was there.

Fu realized he was still holding the herb pouch. He untied the cord that kept it closed and dumped the contents onto a bed of damp leaves next to the cub's head. Fu didn't recognize all of the items, but there was one thing he noticed immediately: bloodmoss. He had no idea if it would work on a tiger, but he figured it couldn't hurt to try.

Fu quickly searched the ground and found two rocks that would serve his purpose. As fast as he could manage, he pounded, lubricated, and applied the healing paste. To his surprise, the cub's panting slowed after he plugged the first wound. The bloodmoss seemed to work for the cub, just like it worked for him. After he patched up the second wound, the cub's eyes rolled back to their normal position, and the cub stared at him as if trying to tell him something. Fu leaned his face in close to the cub's face, their noses nearly touching. The cub's raspy tongue rolled slowly out of its mouth, and Fu saw a thin line of blood lazily run out of a small cut near the tongue's tip. Fu did his best not to flinch as the rough tongue slid up the side of his right cheek, tearing open a small section of the long cut from Ying's chain whip. Fu knew in his heart that the cub's grateful thank-you had just made them blood brothers. The cub seemed to know it, too. It blinked three times in quick succession, then closed its eyes and drifted off to sleep.

Now what? Fu thought. He couldn't just leave the cub there in the middle of the forest. But at the same time, he couldn't stay there himself with no food and no shelter. He decided to take the cub with him in search of the hunters' camp. He figured the cub could use some nourishment, too. Fu reached down and grabbed both of the cub's front paws with one hand. The cub didn't wake, so he took its back paws in his other hand, squatted down, and hoisted the sleeping cub across his shoulders. Then he stood.

The cub was larger up close than it appeared from a distance, but it was lighter than Fu thought it would be. He had no trouble carrying it to the clearing with the pit. Once there, he walked in concentric circles looking for the hunters' tracks, eventually finding two sets: an older set leading to the clearing and a fresher set leading away. Fu chose the older set and started tracing the hunters' steps backward. After some time, they came upon the hunters' abandoned camp in a grassy area. It seemed the hunters had left the pit and headed directly back to their village without returning to the camp. Still, they hadn't left much at the camp. In fact, the only thing they'd left was a smoldering fire.

But the glowing embers gave Fu an idea. He laid the sleeping cub down on a soft patch of grass near the fire pit and searched around until he'd collected enough dry wood to rekindle the flames. He and the cub might not be able to eat right now, but at least he could get dry, and they both could get a little rest. After building up the fire, Fu removed his dripping robe and pants and hung them across several forked branches near the fire. Then he sat down next to the cub and unrolled the wet scrolls to dry them out. He laid them upside down, partially to keep them from rolling back up and partially to keep himself from reviewing them. He was anxious to take a look at them, but he knew he really needed some rest. He would have time to look at the scrolls later.

Fu finished smoothing out the scrolls, then lay down near the cub, next to the warm fire. The cub began to snore, just like Fu often did. Fu looked over and saw that the cub was sleeping with its mouth open, drooling. He often did that, too. As Fu lay there, he realized that these weren't the only things he and the tiger cub had in common. There was also kung fu. Tiger-style kung fu, which was a blending of human skills and tiger skills. That made him and the tiger members of the same spiritual family tree.

And there was something else. Something significant. He and the cub were both orphans. Both without families. Both alone.

Fu recalled the boy he had attacked earlier. That boy was lucky. His father might have pressured him to kill the cub, but in the end, his father didn't make him do it. Also, his father seemed to truly care for him. The boy's father might be a good man, after all. Fu's mind began to race again.

What had he done to the boy? His actions were no better than those of an animal. He had let the animal half of him take control. The only way to make things right was for his other half to get involved. The human half. The man half. A real man admits when he makes a mistake and apologizes, regardless of the consequences. Fu had come to learn this the hard way.

On more than one occasion, he had attacked one or more of his brothers after they offended him or played a small trick on him. His reactions were always far more drastic than the original actions, usually leaving his brother or brothers in bad shape. Afterward, Grandmaster always made Fu swallow his pride and apologize. His brothers had always accepted his apology, and that was that. All was forgotten. Perhaps if he apologized to the boy, he would be forgiven. And maybe if he openly forgave the men for killing the tiger, the men would forgive him for attacking them. If they were good men, they would forgive him.

Grandmaster had told him to find good men to help against Ying. If the hunters were good men, they would help. And if they were very good men, they would also give him some food. At the very least, he could ask the men to direct him to the village dump, where he might be allowed to scavenge for scraps. He was *that* hungry.

Curled up by the fire next to his new blood brother, Fu drifted off to sleep.

CHAPTER 15

"**M**ajor Ying, I have returned!" announced Captain Yue ceremoniously.

Ying pulled his head out of a rain barrel near the Cangzhen main gate and wiped his face on the sleeve of the clean robe he had just put on. Captain Yue paraded over to the opposite side of the rain barrel atop his brown stallion, his immaculate silk robes shimmering in the evening sun.

Ying's third-in-command was a tall man, but he was slight of build, so he usually wore billowing robes to give himself a bulkier appearance. He also wore large, impractical hats to make himself feel important. He wasn't much of a soldier, but he commanded respect nonetheless. He was the Emperor's nephew.

"Why are you back already?" Ying scowled as he cleaned one of his ears with a long fingernail.

"I am happy to report that I have completed my mission," Captain Yue said proudly, adjusting his hat.

Ying pulled his finger from his ear. "What did you just say?"

"I am happy to report that I have completed my mission . . . sir."

Ying's eyes sparkled and he laughed. "You surprise me, Captain Yue. That was quick! Where are your men?"

Captain Yue puffed out his chest. "They're still on the trail, sir. I raced here to give you the news myself. I must say, I've had an exhausting day."

"I can only imagine," Ying replied. "I suppose your men are transporting the young monk. Do you have the scrolls with you? Or are they with your men, too?"

Captain Yue paused. He shifted in his saddle.

"I . . . aaah . . . thought my mission was simply to find a village and inform their most senior official of your search for the young monks and the scrolls."

Ying's face darkened. His eyes no longer sparkled. Now they glowered.

"That's all you've done?" Ying shouted. "And you're *happy* to report it? You're an idiot!"

"You're right, sir," Captain Yue mumbled. "I am a complete idiot. I am sorry. Perhaps, though, you will be at least somewhat pleased to learn that the village I found is home to the Governor of this entire region."

"The Governor?" Ying said, stepping off to the side

of the rain barrel. "You don't say? How did he respond to my edict?"

Captain Yue coughed. "He . . . was, aaah . . . he, was—"

"You didn't even speak to him?" Ying snarled. "You arrogant, good for nothing—"

"I am sorry, sir! I *couldn't* tell him. He wasn't there. He was out hunting tigers. I directed one of his villagers to give him the information when he returns."

"He was hunting *tigers*?" Ying said. "And you didn't go find him? We are on a tiger hunt of our own, Captain Yue."

Captain Yue sighed. "It would take days to find the Governor in this forest, sir."

Ying popped his knuckles, one at time. "You could have tried looking for smoke from a campfire."

"I did, sir. I already thought of that. But we only saw smoke from one campfire, and it was at midday."

"And you didn't investigate?" Ying asked.

Captain Yue looked bewildered. "No, of course not," he said. "Tiger hunters *hunt* during the day, Major Ying. They don't build their fires until their evening meal. Everyone knows that."

"FOOL!" Ying shrieked. "Who do you suppose might build a fire in the middle of the forest in the middle of the day?"

Captain Yue leaned back in his saddle. "I'm sorry, sir. I don't know."

"Perhaps a young monk who spent some time in a water barrel might build a fire to dry out his clothes? IDIOT!"

Ying leaped forward with his arms spread wide like a bird of prey. In midair, he pivoted his waist and cocked his right leg back, preparing to unleash his fury upon Captain Yue. But Captain Yue's stallion sensed what was coming. The horse reared up on its hind legs and pawed wildly at the air with its wickedly sharp front hooves. Ying immediately pulled up short on his attack and floated back to earth. As soon as he hit the ground, he raced around to the backside of the horse and jumped again. But once again the horse sensed what Ying was doing. At just the right moment, the horse let loose a vicious kick with both back legs. Ying twisted sideways, barely escaping permanent injury. He landed on his feet and took a step back, glaring at the horse.

Someone shouted, "Major Ying!"

It was Tonglong. Ying kept his eyes glued to Captain Yue's horse and spoke sharply without turning around.

"Tonglong! What are you doing back already? Are all my leaders incompetent?"

Tonglong trotted forward atop his own stallion. "I have returned because my mission is complete," he replied.

"Ha!" Ying jeered, turning to face Tonglong. "Captain Yue said that very same thing! But he has proven himself to be an idiot who can't follow simple instructions. What you claim is impossible. It should have taken you several days, not one."

Tonglong patted his horse's thick black neck. "I

have the fastest stallion in all China," he said. "Besides, I didn't have to go all the way to the Emperor's palace."

Ying's eyes narrowed. "Don't you dare tell me you didn't speak with the Emperor directly?"

"Of course I spoke with him directly," Tonglong replied. "The Emperor happened to be on a hunting trip in our direction. The Emperor is most pleased with your success, Major Ying."

"Success? Our job isn't finished! Nothing seems to get finished around here. Now leave me be so that I can finish off this horse. At least one thing will have been accomplished today."

Captain Yue coughed. His horse snorted.

Tonglong adjusted his long braid. "Sir, if I may be so bold—I succeeded in completing my mission well beyond expectations. Perhaps this is accomplishment enough for all of us for one day. Please, don't kill the horse. You know that horses are worth their weight in gold out here. Especially the horse before you. It's a real fighter. I suggest you have Captain Yue take it out of your sight if it has offended you in some manner."

Ying looked sideways at Tonglong and grunted. Then he turned to Captain Yue's horse. It reared up once more. Ying spit on it and backed away.

Out of the corner of his eye, Ying spotted movement through the open compound gate. Across the grassy expanse, a single leaf fluttered on a bush near the tree line. There was no breeze.

"Come ON!" Fu said to the tiger cub. "The sun will be setting soon."

The cub didn't budge. It stared up the well-worn trail.

Fu grunted. "We've got to keep moving. I know you're exhausted, but we spent far too much time napping."

The cub stuck its nose high into the air.

"Why are you being so arrogant? If you . . ." Fu's voice trailed off. He smelled it, too. Garbage. And garbage meant humans.

The cub's nose recoiled.

"Let's go!" Fu whispered. "I know it stinks, but maybe we'll get lucky and there will be some fresh table scraps or something. I'm *starving*."

The tiger's ears suddenly perked up. And then Fu heard something, too. Voices. The cub growled.

"Shhh!" Fu said. He moved off the trail.

Fu took a few steps toward the voices and looked over his shoulder to see the cub still sitting on the trail. Staring straight at him, the cub blinked three times, then it turned and walked back the way they had come.

Fu sighed. He was disappointed, but he understood. The cub wanted nothing to do with the hunters they were tracking. He would miss the cub. He hoped he would see his new blood brother again.

Fu adjusted his robe and got down on his hands and knees. He felt a draft on his backside, and his head slumped. *What did I ever do to deserve this?* Fu thought. He adjusted his torn pants as best he could and crawled off through the underbrush, following his nose.

After a few moments, Fu reached one side of an enormous pile of waste. The voices were on the other side. The pile was five times as big as the one at Cangzhen, and it stank a hundred times worse. At Cangzhen, the bulk of their pile was vegetable trimmings. Fu wondered what had been discarded on this one. He doubted he could stomach eating anything that had been left there, no matter how clean the scraps appeared to be.

Fu kneeled down behind a large tree, holding his nose as two men carried on a conversation on the opposite side of the pile. One of them took a bite out of something. It sounded like an apple.

"What a shame it is to waste all this fine food," the man mumbled, his mouth full. "But what else can we do? He told us to dump it, so we've got to dump it. I'm not about to argue with him."

"Nor I, nor I," said the second man. "Dump it, dump it."

Fu sat straight up. He poked his head around the tree.

"Yeah," said the first man, chomping away, "there's no point in making him feel any worse. If I were him, I'd have canceled the celebration, too. Imagine, your only son attacked by a vicious killer monk for no reason. And on top of everything else that's already happened."

"Yes, yes," replied the second man. "So true, so true."

The first man swallowed, then took another bite. "It couldn't have happened to a nicer boy, either," he mumbled. "They say he's now deaf in that ear. Can you imagine?"

"What a shame, what a shame," said the second man.

Fu's eyes widened. He crept out from behind the tree and approached the back side of the pile.

"Yes, it certainly is a shame," said the first man, swallowing. "You don't suppose this killer monk is a friend of that Major Ying? I heard he was once a monk, too, and I know for a fact he's the most evil creature to walk our countryside in generations."

"You never know, you never know," said the second man.

"I bet they're friends. This killer monk is probably trying to make a name for himself, just like that Major Ying has. What is this world coming to? I would do just about anything to stop that Major Ying. He's a villain if I ever saw one."

"Indeed, indeed."

Fu's face flushed. He couldn't believe what he was hearing. He eased his way around the garbage pile.

"Well, are you ready to help me dump this?" the first man asked. "Or are you going to just stand around all day jabbering? I've got things to do and—"

Fu approached the men. He had to say something.

The first man twitched, dropping his apple. It landed in a large cart overflowing with food. "Who . . . who . . . who are you?" he asked, staring at Fu's orange robe.

Fu glanced at the cart, then looked the man in the eye. "I am Fu."

"F-F-Fu?" the man replied nervously. "That's Cantonese, right? Doesn't it mean 'tiger'?"

"Yes," Fu replied.

"You're a t-t-tiger?"

"Sometimes," Fu said. "Other times I'm a regular person. A person who makes mistakes. I have made a mistake, and I've come to apologize. Don't be nervous."

Fu's eyes wandered back to the cart, then he

looked at the second man. The man shuffled his feet.

Fu cleared his throat. "I am the monk who attacked the boy, but I am not a vicious killer, and I'm not a friend of Ying's. I can prove it."

"That's okay! That's okay!" said the second man, backing away.

"I'm not going to harm you," Fu said. He raised his empty hands above his head. "Please listen. I attacked the boy and the hunters in the forest out of anger. I was angry that they killed a mother tiger. I made a big mistake by hitting the boy, and I've come to apologize. If you would be so kind as to take me to him, I would be very grateful. So grateful that I'll share a secret with you. Not only am I not a friend of Ying's, but I also want to stop him. And I have just thought of a plan to do it. You see, I have something that he wants very badly. We could use it as bait to set a trap. What do you think?"

The second man didn't respond. Fu turned to the first man.

"Aaah . . . people don't usually let me think around here," the first man said. "The Governor, on the other hand—he is very good at thinking. Why don't my friend and I go get him? You can wait here. I've noticed you eyeing the food. Why don't you have some? Have it all, in fact. We were just going to dump it, anyway."

Fu leaned toward the cart and his mouth watered. "Are you sure?"

"Absolutely. Take your time. Enjoy. It will be a little

107

while before we find the Governor and bring him here. Relax. I only wish I had some drink to offer you."

"You are too kind," Fu said in his most polite voice. "Please don't fret about the drink. You already do me too many favors. I will wait here for your return."

"Good idea, good idea," the second man said, nodding. "We'll be back, we'll be back."

The two men turned and walked swiftly toward the village.

Fu strutted up to the cart, proud of himself. He'd handled himself like a perfect gentleman and look what it had gotten him! A fine meal and a meeting with the Governor. What luck! Who would have guessed the Governor lived in this very village? If he could win the favor of the Governor, the Gentleman and his son would be sure to forgive him. Plus, if the Governor felt the same way the two villagers did about Ying, he could ask the Governor to help him set a trap.

As Fu reveled in his good fortune, he began to think about the tiger cub. He wished it had stayed with him. They could be enjoying this food together right now.

Fu rummaged through the cart, and his heart leaped. It was filled with delicacies he rarely encountered: beef, pork, lamb, duck, goose, fish, and, best of all, chicken. Buddhist monks were normally not allowed to eat any type of meat, but the warrior monks of Cangzhen had been granted special permission by a powerful emperor hundreds of years earlier. Still, it was rare when any type of meat made its way onto the Cangzhen dining table. Fu dug in.

Quite some time passed, and Fu had finished nearly half the food in the cart when he heard a twig snap behind the pile. *Could that be the cub?* he wondered. It had to be! The villagers would have come from the other direction. Fu was so excited, he nearly dropped the whole roast chickens he held, one in each hand. Engorged, he waddled around the pile to share his good fortune. Fu kept one eye on the tree line looking for the cub and the other on the two slippery chickens. He should have kept both eyes on the tree line. By the time Fu saw the net, it was too late.

CHAPTER 17

"What do they feed it?" the boy asked his mother.

"I have no idea," she said.

"Well, they put it in a cage built for a tiger, right? So maybe they feed it chickens. I heard all tigers love chicken."

"He's a monk, dear. Monks don't eat meat."

"*He's* a vegetarian? He's *huge*! What did they feed him at the temple, *trees*?"

Fu growled at the boy through the bars of the bamboo cage. The boy squealed and ran off. His mother shook her head and walked away after him. But another child stepped right up with a parent in tow. And so it continued as the sun sank in the distance, a seemingly endless parade of people walking past the large cage in the village square. The line was so long, it ran past the bun vendor's shop—the only building visible through the thick wall of bushes and trees that lined the perimeter of the square.

The villagers had come to see the vicious killer monk. It was said he'd put up quite a fight after they'd caught him in the heavy net near the village dump. Men were clawed. Bones were broken. Still, the young wildcat was no match for twenty men and a net. Eventually, they'd restrained him and taken four ancient scrolls from the folds of his robe. Once the men had the scrolls, all the fight went out of the young monk. From that point on, he had been a pussycat.

"I'm not afraid of him!" announced the next boy in line. His name was Ma. He was twelve years old, but he looked like he was at least fourteen or fifteen. He was huge. His hair was long, thick, and unruly. His eyes were like stone. Ma stared at Fu and rolled up the sleeves of his tattered gray robe. Fu stared back.

Ma picked up a rock and threw it at Fu, who sat cross-legged with the backs of his hands resting on his knees, his palms open to the heavens. Fu's right hand flew up and caught the rock a fraction of a second before it hit his head. He slowly lowered his hand back to his knee, the rock resting peacefully in his open palm. The entire time, Fu's head had remained straight, his chin perpendicular to the ground. His eyes never strayed from Ma's.

"Oh, you think you're tough?" Ma asked. "Catch this!" He gathered several rocks and unleashed them all simultaneously in Fu's direction. Fu's left arm remained relaxed while his right arm became a blur of motion, stopping as abruptly as it had started. When Fu returned his hand to his knee and opened his fingers, several rocks rolled out. Fu's eyes never wavered from Ma's.

Ma was amazed, but also infuriated.

"That's it!" Ma yelled. "I'll kick your fat—"

"Enough!" shouted a familiar voice. The long line of children and parents broke up as the Gentleman from the forest approached with his son trailing behind.

"Go home, all of you!" the Gentleman shouted. "You should have more important things to do than waste your time eyeing a beast in a cage!"

As the crowd dispersed, the Gentleman's son sat on the ground, far from the cage. The Gentleman approached Ma, his rich green robe shimmering in the evening light. The Gentleman glared at Ma.

"I saw that," he said.

"I'm sorry, Governor," Ma replied softly. He looked away.

Governor? Fu thought. *Oh, no!*

"You should be sorry," the Governor said. "Nothing good comes to people who act the way you just did."

Ma put his head down. The Governor put his hand on Ma's shoulder and lowered his voice. "Listen, would you do me a small favor? Could you please keep Ho occupied while I talk to the animal in the cage? Ho isn't feeling too well, understandably."

"Sure," Ma whispered. He walked over to Ho's side and sat down. Ma playfully punched one of Ho's skinny arms. Ho ignored him. Ma smiled and leaned over to whisper in one of Ho's ears, then stopped. He scooted over to Ho's other side and whispered into that one instead.

The Governor turned toward Fu.

"So, Beast Child," he said. "What do you have to say for yourself?"

Fu lowered his eyes. "I am sorry, sir. I am very truly sorry, and I wish to apologize to your son."

"Do you, now?" the Governor replied. "And what purpose would that serve?"

"Aaah . . . ," Fu said, looking up. "Perhaps it will make him feel better?"

"Perhaps it will make *him* feel better, you say? Do you really think so?"

"I suppose so," Fu replied. "Sure. I know it would make me feel a lot better."

"Ah, yes," the Governor said. "It is all about *you,* is it not?"

"Please, sir," Fu said. "I only wish to apologize. That's why I came here. To apologize and to tell you about the scrolls. Also, I think I was meant to come here. The men I spoke to at the waste pile said that they wanted to get rid of Major Ying. I do, too, and I have a plan! If we use the scrolls as bait, we could—"

"Stop!" said the Governor, raising his hand. "There is no point in talking further. I have already sent messengers to Major Ying. I have promised the scrolls to him, and I am a man of my word."

"What?" Fu cried. He grabbed the bamboo bars. "Are you crazy?"

"Watch your mouth, young man!" the Governor said, leaning forward. "Do you not realize to whom you are speaking?"

"I do . . . I'm sorry . . . it's just that you don't seem to understand . . . you don't realize that—"

"I only need to realize one thing," the Governor said, turning away from Fu. "You put us in much danger. You attacked my men and my son unprovoked, and you have a habit of stealing things from important people like Major Ying. If you were to stay here, who knows what you might steal from me? Major Ying has asked for the return of his scrolls and your capture. He reports directly to the Emperor, so it is my duty to honor his wishes."

"No!" cried Fu. "You can't! Those scrolls aren't even his! He tried to steal them from Cangzhen Temple! *My* temple! If you would just listen to me, you'll see that—"

The Governor spun back toward Fu. "That is enough, young man! I see only as far as the region I govern, and you bring trouble to my region. Therefore, you must go. And now, so must I."

The Governor turned to his son. "Come," he said. "It's time to go home, Ho."

And with that, the Governor turned and walked away, his son at his side.

"Please, wait!" Fu cried out. "I thought you were a good man! I have more to say!"

But no one listened.

CHAPTER 18

116

At first, Fu thought he was seeing things. Darkness had begun to settle in, and he was under a lot of stress. Perhaps his mind was playing tricks on him. But— there it was again! Across the square a huge basket of rice seemed to move. And then it stood!

In front of the bun vendor's shop, a large, heavyset man lifted the battered remnants of an old rice basket off his head and shoulders. Fu realized he must have sat down and covered himself with it to keep dew from forming on him as night set in. Fu hadn't noticed it there before.

The big man swayed slightly. Long tangles of matted black hair hung partway down his back and forward over his face, intertwined with his long, scraggly beard. His pants and robe were filthy. The man raised his beefy arms and stretched, yawning. Then he began to stumble forward, as though drunk. He stopped several paces from Fu's cage and stood there, weaving back and forth. He stared at Fu between strands of hair. Fu thought he saw something familiar in the man's eyes, but he wasn't sure what.

Fu shook his head and rubbed his eyes. He must be seeing things.

The Drunkard spoke with a deep, gravelly voice.

"What is your name?"

"Fu."

The Drunkard paused. One eyebrow raised up. "Who would give you the name *Tiger*?"

"My temple's Grandmaster."

"Your name is Cantonese," the Drunkard said, stumbling closer. "But Canton is very far from here. What temple are you from?"

Fu folded his arms. "What do you care?"

"What do you care that I care?"

Fu cocked his head to one side. "Why do you answer my question with a question?"

"Why are you so reluctant to answer?"

Fu leaned back, frustrated. "You talk like a monk, you filthy bum."

"Perhaps that is because I've spent some time with monks," the Drunkard said, smiling.

"Sure you have."

"Surely, I have," the Drunkard said.

Fu sneered. "Next you're going to tell me that the

monks you spent time with were from the great Shaolin Temple, right?" Fu leaned forward.

The Drunkard leaned forward, too. "Perhaps," he said. The Drunkard lost his balance and stumbled into the cage. It shook violently.

Fu leaned back. "You're pathetic. You only say that because Shaolin is so famous, even a lowly, homeless Drunkard would have heard of it. What would you know about Shaolin?"

The Drunkard brushed his tangled hair to the side. "I know that the monks there never attack innocent villagers."

Fu banged his fists against the front of the cage. "That's not fair! I said I was sorry!"

The hair fell back over the Drunkard's eyes. He continued to stare but said nothing more.

"What more can I do?" Fu asked. "I made a mistake, but I am not entirely at fault. Those hunters should share some of the blame."

"Really?" the Drunkard asked.

"Really!" Fu said. "Listen to what I have to say, Drunkard, since no one else in this stupid village will. I am a Cangzhen monk. My temple was secret, founded by Shaolin monks who fought for Truth and defended Justice. We were recently attacked and our temple was destroyed by a traitor, and I've been sent to find others to help me stop the traitor before he ruins even more lives. That traitor is none other than Major Ying. In my search for help, I happened across some men hunting tigers for sport, one of whom was the Governor. As a Cangzhen monk, I cannot stand around while tigers are destroyed for no reason."

"No reason?" the Drunkard said. "Did the hunters tell you that they were only hunting for sport?"

"They didn't say that they weren't," Fu replied.

"Perhaps you should have asked them what they were doing before you attacked."

"I *saw* what they were doing!" Fu said.

"Not everything is the way it looks, young man," the Drunkard said in a fatherly tone. "Sometimes you need to listen, too. You've said it yourself."

Fu slammed his fist down on the floor of the cage. "They had nothing to say!"

"Really?" the Drunkard asked.

"Really!"

"Tell me then, monk—what do you think of the Governor?"

Fu rolled his eyes. "He is a fool."

"Really?"

"Really! Really! Really!" Fu said, slamming his fist down again. "A thousand times, really! Only a fool would promise those scrolls to Ying."

The Drunkard scratched his scraggly beard. "How is the Governor to know what Major Ying might do with the scrolls?"

"I was *trying* to tell him!" Fu replied. "All the Governor had to do was listen to me for a second."

"So you're saying that anyone who doesn't listen to you is a fool?"

"Yes! I mean, no!" Fu took a deep breath and

paused. "What I mean is, anyone who doesn't listen in general is a fool."

"Okay, that's fair," the Drunkard said. He sat down on the ground in front of Fu. "I have something to say, then. Are you listening?"

Fu rolled his eyes again but kept his mouth closed and his ears open.

"The Governor's wife was killed by that tiger you saw in the pit this morning," the Drunkard said.

"What!" Fu shouted. "Why would you say such a thing?"

"I say it because it is true," the Drunkard replied. "And remember Ho, the boy you attacked? She was Ho's mother."

"How . . . how do you know this to be true?" Fu asked. He felt dizzy.

"I saw some things and heard many more. But you can decide for yourself. Did the tiger in the pit have a broken spear in its shoulder? A decorated spear?"

"Yes, it did," Fu said. "One of the hunters must have stabbed it while it was in the pit."

"No. That is not necessarily true. You see, several days ago Ho and his mother and father were out near the forest's edge looking for wild mushrooms, and a tiger attacked Ho's mother without warning. The Governor happened to be carrying one of his fancy spears to scare off thieves, and as the beast dragged his wife away, he bravely ran up and sank the spear deep into the tiger's shoulder. This I saw with my very own eyes, having been drawn to the scene by Ho's cries. I ran up to help the Governor, and the spear broke. The wounded tiger released the woman and fled with its cub, but it was too late. Ho's mother's spirit never made it out of the forest."

Fu couldn't believe his ears. However, the look in the Drunkard's eyes told him that the man was telling the truth. His dizziness grew worse.

"Once a tiger has hunted a human," the Drunkard said, "it will very likely do so again. Especially if it is wounded or lame like this one was with the spear in its shoulder. Even more so if it has a cub to feed. So you see, the Governor had no choice but to hunt down the tiger."

Fu lowered his eyes.

"And here's something else you should know," the Drunkard said. "The cage in which you now sit was not built to keep the tigers from getting out; it was built to keep the villagers from getting in. The plan was to destroy the mother and its cub and bring their bodies back here to throw in the cage for all to see. These villagers would tear the tigers' bodies to shreds with their teeth, they are so upset about the loss. If not for the cage, they might tear *you* to shreds."

Fu lay down. He was so dizzy now that he could not sit up any longer. To think, he once considered the Governor's son lucky.

"I—I understand why they would be upset with the adult tiger," Fu stammered. "But why kill the cub?"

The Drunkard stood up. "It is said that once a tiger has had a taste of man, it will always be a man-eater.

Perhaps the cub did not bite the Governor's wife, but it saw what its mother did. The Governor did not want to take any chances."

Fu felt nauseous. The cage was spinning fast now, and the food he had devoured earlier rose to the back of his throat. He coughed, struggling to focus on the point where the Drunkard stood. But the Drunkard was no longer there. Fu opened his mouth to say something, but the pressure on the back of his throat was too great. He coughed again. Then he shook his head and closed his eyes.

CHAPTER 19

Ying crouched behind the fire he had built at the front corner of the Cangzhen compound, near the Forgotten Pagoda. He watched his shadow dance on the perimeter wall and listened closely to the sounds of the night. Ever since the young monks had fled Cangzhen, Ying had felt like he was being watched. He couldn't tell where the watcher was positioned, which could only mean one thing. There was only one person alive who could fly this close beneath his nose and not be seen.

Tonglong approached Ying from the opposite side of the large campfire.

"Greetings, sir," Tonglong said. "I hope all is well with you this fine evening."

Ying grunted and stood. He stared over the flames at his number one soldier. "Tell me, Tonglong—since the men seem to think you're so clever—what is the best way to catch a crane?"

Tonglong paused and leaned back on his boot heels. "A crane? You mean the large water bird? I've never hunted one—are they tasty?"

"I don't know," Ying said, turning away. "Perhaps we will find out."

"What do you intend to do?"

Ying took a deep breath. "I sense someone has been watching us for quite some time, and I think it is Hok—one of my former brothers."

"One of the young monks?" Tonglong said. "Commander Woo and the men seem certain we're being watched by restless spirits."

"Commander Woo is a superstitious fool."

Tonglong rubbed his strong jaw. "He is what he is, Major Ying. If you want to change his mind—and the minds of the men—you'll need to catch this Hok."

"I don't care about changing anyone's mind," Ying scowled, pivoting around to face Tonglong. "I only want to catch Hok."

"I see," Tonglong said. "May I ask you a question, sir?"

Ying grunted.

"Perhaps it is because I'm Cantonese, but I'm curious about something. *Hok* is the Cantonese word for 'crane'; likewise *Ying* is the Cantonese word for 'eagle.' Why do you Cangzhen monks have Cantonese names? Your temple was not in Canton. Everyone in this region speaks Mandarin Chinese—including you."

Ying frowned. "Grandmaster was from Canton. He wanted to keep the temple secret, so he gave us all Cantonese names and taught us to speak Cantonese as a second language. If we were ever away from the temple, we were supposed to speak Cantonese and pretend that we were just passing through the area."

Tonglong's eyebrows raised. "You were supposed to lie?"

"Yes," Ying replied.

"But *Cangzhen* means 'hidden truth,' does it not?"

"Yes."

Tonglong looked off to one side. "It seems odd that your temple is called *truth,* but you were asked to lie."

"I know," Ying said, watching Tonglong closely.

"What was the big secret?"

"Grandmaster never told us," replied Ying, his eyes still glued to Tonglong. "But I have my suspicions. Why are you so curious?"

"I'm just making conversation," Tonglong said, glancing over at Ying. "Also, I find it interesting. I am sorry if I have offended you."

"I appreciate your curiosity," Ying said. "But I have trouble trusting people."

"If you do not trust people, you make them untrustworthy," Tonglong said.

"I know that!" Ying snapped. "It's an old Buddhist proverb. But proverbs mean nothing to me. They are just words. Actions have far more meaning than words."

Tonglong folded his hands. "But words can change a person's heart."

"So can actions!" Ying raised a fist. "But I doubt you would understand my position."

"I might," Tonglong said calmly. "I have been through quite a bit myself."

"Really?" Ying said, leaning forward. "My entire family is dead."

"Mine, too," Tonglong replied.

"Oh? What about friends? Did you ever have a best friend?"

"Yes, once," Tonglong said.

"Did he die?" Ying spat. *"Right in front of you?"*

"Actually, yes," Tonglong said.

"I don't believe it," said Ying, looking away.

"Believe it or don't, that is your choice. I will tell you about it, if you would like to listen."

"I don't care about your experiences!" Ying said. "And I no longer feel like talking!"

Tonglong responded respectfully, "Sir, I did not come over here expecting a conversation. I came over only to say hello. But since we're talking, I would greatly appreciate it if you would answer one or two more questions. For the men—I will pass the information along."

Ying nodded once.

Tonglong tapped his chin. "I know that the large young monk called Fu escaped with his life, and now you've mentioned one called Hok. That is two. What are the names of the three?"

"Malao, Seh, and Long."

"Monkey, Snake, Dragon?" Tonglong said. "Are all Cangzhen monks named after animals?"

"No," Ying said. "Just those five are, plus myself. There was a seventh, but he is no more."

Tonglong's head tilted to one side. "What was his name?"

Ying paused, closing his eyes. "His name was Luk."

"*Deer?*" Tonglong asked, surprised.

"Yes!" Ying said, opening his eyes. "Do you have a problem with that?"

"I am sorry, sir," Tonglong said in a sincere tone. "Please do not be offended by this, but I can't imagine a deer being a very dangerous fighter. They're so . . . timid."

"You would not question the style if you'd ever seen Luk in action!" Ying sneered. "He was unbeatable with antler knives in his hands."

"Again, I am sorry, sir." Tonglong paused, staring into the fire. "Your voice is filled with sadness and anger. Why?"

"Luk was my best friend," Ying replied.

"How did he die?" Tonglong asked, looking up. "Was it some kind of accident?"

"It was no accident!" Ying shouted, suddenly bursting with energy. His eyes glowered at Tonglong from the opposite side of the fire. "It was all Grandmaster's fault! Grandmaster took a group of us on a mission for the new Emperor. We killed hundreds. The Emperor wanted to reward us handsomely, but Grandmaster refused to accept anything for our efforts. The Emperor noticed my frustration and offered me a special reward if I would do him a favor. The favor required two people, so Luk came with me. Things went wrong, and Luk died."

"Pardon me for asking, Major Ying, but how does that make the Grandmaster responsible?"

"If Grandmaster had accepted the reward and distributed it to each of us as the Emperor had offered, I would never have accepted the Emperor's request—because there would have *been* no request! Then my best friend would still be alive!"

Tonglong said nothing.

"Another way to look at it is this," Ying snarled. "If Grandmaster hadn't gone to the Emperor's aid in the first place, Luk would still be alive. Or if Grandmaster hadn't chosen me and Luk to go along, Luk would still be alive. Do you see my point?"

Tonglong closed his eyes.

"Look at me when I'm talking to you!" Ying shouted, baring his razor-sharp teeth. "How dare you respond this way? Do you have feelings for Grandmaster?"

"No!" Tonglong said. His head twitched slightly.

"What was that?" Ying said.

"What was what?"

"That twitch—" Ying said, leaning forward and staring over the flames. "Your head, it—"

"I have no idea what you're talking about!"

"Don't raise your voice to me!" Ying shouted. He leaped over the fire, his arms spread wide. He landed in front of Tonglong. "You know what? Now that I think about it, I didn't see you slay a single monk in our attack on Cangzhen. Do you have some kind of tie to Cangzhen? To Grandmaster? What are you up to, Cantonese man!"

"Don't be ridiculous," Tonglong said, turning away. "During the attack, I stayed back in order to watch our men in action. As your number one soldier, that is part of my job."

"I'm not sure I believe you," Ying said. "Remind me why it is that I selected you as my number one."

"You chose me for my loyalty," Tonglong said, turning back to face Ying. "And for my fighting skills."

"I chose you for your fighting skills," Ying replied. "I know nothing of your loyalties. I am beginning to get suspicious of you."

"Suspicious? Whatever for? Did I not prove my loyalty by handing over my family sword when you asked for it earlier?"

"You did, but you hesitated. Also, you returned far too quickly from your delivery assignment to the Emperor."

"Sir," Tonglong said, standing straight. "What can I do to prove myself to you?"

"Catch me a crane."

"Done."

CHAPTER 20

Fu woke to the warm sun on his face and the smell of freshly baked buns wafting through the air. He felt refreshed and extraordinarily pleasant as he thought about the wonderful breakfast he would soon have. Freshly baked buns weren't often served at Cangzhen, and he couldn't wait to dig in. As he listened to his brothers' anxious voices in the distance, he realized something. Those weren't his brothers' voices.

Fu opened his eyes and saw bamboo bars all around him. He sat up and remembered where he was. Then he remembered what he had come to the village to do. Fu paid close attention to the two voices moving quickly along the far side of the tall hedge bordering the village square.

"Come on!" Ma said. "Let's GO!"

"No, thanks," Ho replied. "I don't feel like it."

"Trust me, it will make you feel ten times better."

"I don't think so."

"It will make you feel one hundred times better!"

"I doubt it."

"How do you know unless you try?"

"Just leave me alone, okay?"

"No way. You're coming with me."

Fu heard scuffling. Someone grunted.

"You're hurting me," Ho said.

"Quit complaining," Ma replied. "We're almost there."

Fu sat up when he saw the boys approaching, the large one with the smaller one draped over his shoulder. Ma set Ho down in front of the cage and stood beside him.

"Watch," Ma said. He inhaled deeply through his nose, making a tremendous noise as he constricted his windpipe just the right amount. A wad of thick mucus was slowly drawn out of his nose and into the back of his throat. With his windpipe still constricted, Ma forced air out of his lungs and popped the wad out of his throat and into his mouth. Then he raised his lower lip up to contain the glob and spoke slowly as a line of saliva slipped out, running down his chin.

"Catch this, monk," he slurred.

Ma closed his mouth around the lump and pursed his lips. He inhaled deeply through his nose, curled his tongue, and let it fly.

Fu didn't flinch. He watched as the glob hit one of the bamboo cage bars, sticking briefly before oozing slowly downward.

"So close!" Ma said, wiping his mouth across his robe's gray sleeve. "I think I have enough ammo for one more shot—"

"Excuse me," Fu interrupted. "May I say something?"

Ma pointed his finger at Fu and glared. "You don't have anything to say that I'm interested in hearing."

"With all due respect," Fu said politely, "I don't have anything to say to you. I have something to say to Ho. It will only take a moment."

"I don't think—" Ma began to say.

"Let him talk," Ho interrupted, stepping forward. "I'd like to hear what he has to say."

Ma nodded his head. "Let's hear it then, monk."

"I am very sorry I attacked you," Fu said, looking directly at Ho. He folded his hands in his lap. "It was wrong, and I sincerely apologize. If you wish to hit me with something, I understand completely. Only I suggest you use an item that transmits force a little better than spit. Take hold of a spear or staff, and I'll place my head between the bars. Hit me as hard as you can."

"No," Ho said, shaking his head. "I don't think so."

"Please," Fu said. "Please, hit me. Treat me as I have treated you. Treat me ten times worse. It will make me feel better. I deserve it."

"It won't make me feel any better," Ho replied. "I don't get pleasure from hurting people."

"I'll hit him!" Ma offered. "It will make me feel better!"

"No," said Ho. "You're not going to hit him."

"Come on," Ma said. "I'll just hit him once. Right in the ear—"

"NO!" Ho said defiantly. He stomped his foot. "No one is going to hit anyone on my account!"

Ma took a few steps back and frowned. Fu recognized the tension in Ho's voice and spoke to him softly. Softer than he had ever spoken to anyone before.

"Okay, Ho," Fu said. "Nobody has to hit anybody. But I would still like to do something for you. How about if I teach you to fight?"

"No!" Ho said, folding his arms. "I don't want to learn how to fight."

"But if you learn how to fight, you can defend yourself against people like me in the future," Fu said. "No one will ever hurt you again."

"No."

"Well," Fu said, "what *do* you want?"

"Wait!" Ma interrupted. "I have an idea! Hey, monk, why don't you teach *me* to fight?"

Fu looked to Ho for a reaction. Ho looked at the ground.

"All right," Fu said, still looking at Ho. "Since you don't want to learn how to fight, I'll teach your friend Ma. Then he can protect you."

"Whatever," said Ho, turning away. He headed for the bun shop across the square.

The sun was still low in the morning sky as Fu and Ma stared at each other through the bars of the bamboo cage. Fu sat cross-legged, his hands on his knees. Ma stood firm and straight.

"*Ma* means 'horse,'" Fu said. "Right?"

Ma rolled up his sleeves. "Yes. So?"

"If your mother named you appropriately, your legs should be quite strong," Fu replied. "Is this true?"

"Yes," Ma said. "What are you trying to say?"

Fu rubbed his bald head, lost in thought. He slapped his right thigh. "I will teach you the No Shadow Kick. If you practice it for ten years, it might make you famous."

"Ten years!" Ma exclaimed.

"Yes, ten years," Fu said, serious. "Maybe a little more, maybe a little less."

Ma's mouth dropped. "I can't wait that long to fight! Teach me something that doesn't take so long."

"All good things take time."

"Well . . . ," Ma said, "then teach me many things so that I can practice all of them for a long time."

"That won't work," Fu replied. "Besides, I have a feeling I won't be here much longer. There's only time to teach you one thing. But that's okay. We had a saying at Cangzhen—*I fear the one kick you've practiced ten thousand times, not the ten thousand kicks you've practiced only once.*"

"Come on," Ma said. "You've got to teach me more than just one kick."

Fu shook his head. "I can't. Ying and his men will be here soon. But perhaps if you find some friends, I can show each of them one different thing, and later you can teach each other your one thing. Then everyone will learn quite a lot. Right?"

"I guess you're right," Ma said. He kicked the dirt. "But you have to teach me my thing first! Then I'll go get some of my friends."

"As you wish," Fu said. "We will begin with the proper stance; it is the foundation for most things. It's called the Horse Stance because it is powerful. Just like a horse. Just like you."

Ma smiled.

"Watch this," Fu said. "Then copy me."

Fu stood and hunched over inside the cage. He

spread his feet shoulder-width apart and squatted way down. When his thighs were parallel to the ground, he straightened his back all the way up and lifted his head so that his neck was in line with his spine. His head didn't hit the top of the cage—which was a relief—but the scratch across his backside began to burn a little. Fu had forgotten all about the scratch, as well as the gaping hole in his clothing. At least when he squatted this far down, no one could see into the hole.

In front of the cage, Ma stood and did his best to copy Fu. Fu noticed that Ma could keep either his back straight or his thighs parallel to the ground. He couldn't do both at the same time without falling over. Ma looked frustrated.

"Don't worry about it," Fu said. "It will take you months to be flexible enough to do it as low as me. Just try to remember how I look, and you'll get there one day. Now, see my hands? Their position is important, too. Copy me. Make a fist with each hand by curling your fingers tightly into your palm. Next, bend your thumb and wrap it over your curled fingers just in front of the big knuckle on your pointer finger. Got it? Now, bend your right arm up ninety degrees and tilt your fist over in front of your face to protect it. Great. Next, put your left arm straight down between your legs and bend your elbow slightly. Use that fist to protect your groin. Most people fight with both hands up in front of their face—until they get kicked in the groin a few times."

Ma giggled. Fu did not. Ma stopped giggling.

"From this position, you should be grounded," Fu said. "Solid as an oak. Your feet should feel rooted to the earth. Immovable. Let all the earth's positive *chi*—positive energy—flow into your body through the soles of your feet, washing your body clean as it travels through your system and out your fists. You should do this at least one hour straight, every single day, for at least one year."

"Do what?" Ma asked. "Just stand here in this position?"

"Yes," Fu said. "This is your foundation. Without a solid foundation, everything will topple over—just as you did when you first tried it. Trust me. But we don't have one year to wait before I teach you more, so I'll go ahead and show you the kick. This is called the No Shadow Kick because it is so fast, it leaves no shadow. Watch."

Fu's body swayed slightly and his robe fluttered. Neither leg seemed to move, but Ma's unruly hair flew back as a whoosh of air rushed over his head. Ma looked around, then looked back at Fu, amazed.

"You felt that breeze, didn't you?" Fu asked.

"Yes, but . . . how did you . . . ?"

"That is the No Shadow Kick. It is very powerful."

"It is magic," Ma said.

"No, it's not magic," Fu replied. "Only hard work. Very hard work. The kick is actually very simple. I just did it really, really fast and strong. Watch again."

This time, Fu did it slowly. It looked so simple.

With his fists locked in position, all he did was shift his weight onto his left leg and bring his right knee up high. With his right foot bent nearly ninety degrees, Fu snapped his leg forward, extending it until it was straight out in front of him, parallel to the ground. His foot was now nearly perpendicular to the ground, and his toes were flexed backward so that any impact would be made with the ball of his foot. Fu repeated the movements slowly in reverse and ended by returning his foot to its original position in the Horse Stance.

"Do you think you've got it?" Fu asked.

Ma nodded his head.

"Good," Fu said. "As you can see, it is a simple front kick. But if you do it fast enough and hard enough, it is nearly impossible to stop. If you find you have to use it anytime soon, I suggest you aim for one of your opponent's knees. If you keep the kick low, you will maintain your balance easier. Also, most people won't expect it low, which makes it very effective. Just don't forget that it is important to stay rooted when you do this or any other kick or punch because you are transmitting energy. If you were to use only the strength of your muscles against an opponent, it would certainly have an effect. But if you stay rooted and pull energy from the whole earth, it will have a much greater effect. Does that make sense?"

"Yes," Ma replied.

Fu nodded his head. "Now, there are two more

things you must always remember. First, you should only fight as a last resort, and only when necessary. All right?"

Ma looked sideways. "Sure."

"Promise me," said Fu.

Ma looked back at Fu. "Okay. I promise."

Fu took a deep breath. "The other thing is perhaps even more important. For every action, there is an equal, opposing reaction. This applies to life, as well as the fighting arts. Do you understand?"

"Yes," Ma said.

"Are you sure?" asked Fu.

"Of course I'm sure," Ma replied, swinging his arms. "Now, is this lesson over? I'm getting hungry."

"The lesson is over whenever you say it is over," Fu said. "I am the one stuck in the cage. You can walk away at any time. However, it was my own teachers' custom to conclude all training sessions with a question from each student. Do you have a question for me?"

Ma scratched his head, then smiled. "Do you like pork inside your steamed breakfast buns, Teacher? Or do you prefer chicken?"

CHAPTER 22

"Major Ying!" Commander Woo shouted. "We have visitors this morning! They bring news of a captured monk!"

Ying stopped sharpening his toenails and looked over at the Cangzhen main gate. Commander Woo and Captain Yue stood just beyond it, side by side. Not to be outdone, Captain Yue added, "The visitors are from the same village I went to, sir! I recognize one of them!"

Ying sighed and stood up from the low bench next to the fire pit. He saw two men in gray peasant's robes come into view. Commader Woo grabbed the arm of the first man and yanked him toward the gate. Captain Yue latched onto the second man, but the man shrugged him off. Captain Yue coughed and adjusted his hat. He remained behind as Commander Woo led the two villagers through the gate.

"What news do you bring?" Ying asked as the men approached. His tongue wriggled inside his mouth and the villagers jumped but did not answer. They both stared at Ying, wide-eyed.

Commander Woo squeezed the first man's arm. The man yelped.

"Answer the question," Commander Woo said.

"We . . . aaah . . . bring news of a captured young monk, Major Ying," the man said, cowering. "And news of your scrolls."

Ying leaned his head to the side. "You have the boy *and* the scrolls?"

"Yes, sir," the man replied, looking down at Ying's feet. He shuddered.

Ying's eyes narrowed. "How many scrolls are there?"

"Four, sir," the villager said.

"And what do they look like?"

The man looked up at Ying, surprised. "No one dared open them, sir. We thought it best to stay out of your business."

Ying grinned. "All right, then, describe the boy."

"He is, well, rather large for his age. He appears to be about twelve years old. He is bald and wears an orange monk's robe. He has a deep, gravelly voice. He—"

"Is there anything wrong with his face?" Ying asked.

The villager paused. "What . . . aaah . . . exactly do you mean by *wrong,* sir?"

"Does he have any distinguishing marks *on his face!*"

"He has a . . . aaah . . . long, handsome scar forming across one cheek. Much like you have, sir."

Ying's carved face grew dark. "Enough! This man appears to be telling the truth." Ying looked over at the gate. Captain Yue was standing there, staring at his reflection in the rain barrel.

"Captain Yue," Ying shouted. "Get over here! Now!"

Captain Yue sprinted over.

Ying rubbed his forehead. "Commander Woo, you still have work to do here, and Tonglong is out on a special mission. I guess I will have to leave this in your hands, Captain Yue. You failed miserably the first time you went to that village. This will be your chance to redeem yourself. Take fifty men and return to the village to collect the young monk and the scrolls. Bring them back here. If you fail again, you will answer to me—and not even your horse will stand between us. Understood?"

"Yes, sir," Captain Yue said. He swallowed hard.

"Well, what are you waiting for?" Ying snarled. "Choose your men, mount that demon stallion of yours, and GO!"

The day was drawing to a close, and the entire village was gathered in the square watching Fu teach nearly one hundred children one kung fu technique each from inside the cage. There were boys and girls alike, each taking a turn standing just outside the cage bars for their personal instruction. Several of the boys complained about girls being involved until Fu told them that he would not teach any of the boys anything if they didn't stop complaining. Moreover, he informed the boys that more than a few women had been "nuns" at temples throughout China, including the famous Shaolin Temple. Fu assured the boys that if they ever crossed paths with a warrior "nun," they would want to be sure to keep their negative thoughts about girls to themselves.

The whole time, there was much talk among the parents as to whether Fu's kung fu course should be stopped immediately—especially with girls involved. However, in the end, most of the parents agreed that since no one had gotten hurt and the kids seemed to be enjoying themselves, the training could continue. The day was warm, and the atmosphere in the square was pleasant. The same could not be said for the atmosphere inside the bun vendor's shop. It was hot in there. Very hot, indeed.

"I say we let him go," one man said. "He's obviously not a bad kid. He just made a mistake."

"Not a bad kid?" another shouted. "Look at poor little Ho! He's been sitting in that corner all day with one ear cocked in our direction because his other one doesn't work!"

Ho stood up and shouted back across the crowded room. "My head has been straight for hours! Not cocked! And I already told you—my hearing is returning!"

The Governor stood and put his hand on Ho's shoulder. The room quieted down. The Governor leaned over.

"What has gotten into you, son? I've never seen you like this before."

Ho plopped back down in his chair. "I've never been this upset before, Father. I hate when people argue, and I really hate when people argue over me.

I'm the one who has suffered most, and I still think we should let the monk go. Just as long as he promises not to attack anyone from our village ever again. What's done is done. Past is past. That's what you always say, isn't it?"

The Governor sat down, facing Ho. He rested his forearms on his knees. "That is very big of you, son. But it's not that simple. There are a lot of politics involved. The main thing is, I've already sent two men to inform Major Ying of the young monk's capture. If soldiers arrive to collect him and he's not here, the soldiers will be very, very angry. So angry, in fact, that they may destroy our entire village. I've seen it before."

A man in the crowd said bitterly, "So what are we going to do, Governor? Just hand the boy over—and sentence him to *death*?"

"Don't be ridiculous!" someone shouted. "We don't know that he will be killed."

"They killed all his brothers and destroyed his entire temple!" another shouted back. "That's what that captain said! I say we let the monk go. If the soldiers give us a hard time, we'll just say that the boy escaped."

"If he 'escapes,' the entire village will be destroyed!"

"You don't know that! You wouldn't know a—"

The voices inside the bun shop grew louder and louder. So loud, in fact, that Fu heard every word. He knew he had to do something to help make things right, but what? He was struggling to come up with a plan when Ma appeared carrying a terra-cotta roasting pot.

"Here," Ma said, forcing the pot between the bars of the cage. "I asked my mother to make this for you. It's her famous Greasy Goose. I also brought you a needle and some thread to fix your robe and your pants."

"Thanks," Fu said. He made a strange face as he reached for the items.

"I know, sewing is woman's work," Ma said. "But you really should cover yourself up better."

Sewing wasn't the reason Fu had made the face. Everyone had a job at Cangzhen, and Fu's happened to be mending everyone else's torn robes and pants. He was actually quite good at it. It was the food that made his face turn sour. Fu removed the lid and winced. Though he loved chicken and even duck, he had problems with goose. Especially Greasy Goose. The one time he'd eaten it, his stomach hadn't been the same for an entire day. Fu put the lid back on the pot and pushed it aside.

"Aaah . . . thank you very much," Fu said. "I'll . . . eat it later."

"Later?" Ma said. "Aren't you hungry? My mother made it just for you, you know. She feels sorry for you. She said no child should ever be locked in a cage."

Fu lowered his eyes. "Please tell your mother I said thank you very much, but . . ."

"But *what*?" Ma asked, irritated.

Just then, the wind picked up and blew the Greasy Goose aroma in Fu's direction. His stomach turned.

"But . . . nothing," Fu said, looking up. He had just thought of a plan. "Please tell your mother I don't know how I'll ever be able to thank her!"

Fu tossed the pot's heavy lid aside and grabbed the entire goose with both hands. He tore into it, eating as fast as his jaws would chew. In no time, his stomach began to grumble loudly. His plan, it seemed, was in motion.

"**G**entlemen, it's time we go home to our families," said the Governor to everyone assembled inside the bun vendor's shop. "We can continue this discussion tomorrow."

"Agreed," said most of the men.

As they filed into the village square, their noses began to recoil. A few men gagged. Something smelled very, very unpleasant.

"Oh, my stomach!" Fu called out. "Owwww. . . ."

The Governor shook his head. He removed a torch that burned outside the shop's front door and walked over to the cage. Several men followed. So did Ho.

"What on earth did you eat, young man?" the

Governor asked Fu as he approached the cage, holding his nose.

"A gift from Ma's mother," Fu replied. He rocked back and forth, his arms wrapped around himself. "I believe Ma called it Greasy Goose. I'm afraid my stomach isn't accustomed to such rich food."

The Governor shook his head. "Tomorrow I might be able to persuade the village pharmacist to mix up a tea to settle your stomach. *If* you continue to behave. But I am afraid you are on your own tonight. There is nothing I can do for you."

"Oh, but there is, sir," Fu said, desperation in his voice. "You could let me empty my sour stomach somewhere."

One of the men stepped forward. "Just take care of your business in the corner of your cage, animal."

"Are you crazy?" another man said. "The whole village will stink until the cage is gone! And do *you* want to be the one to give Major Ying a cage full of foulness?"

"All right, all right," said the Governor, waving the torch. "That's enough bickering. Young monk, do you swear by Buddha that you won't attack anyone tonight?"

"Yes, yes," Fu replied impatiently. "I swear I won't attack anyone tonight. Please, hurry."

The Governor handed the torch to one of the men and unlocked the cage's latch with a key he had hanging around his neck. He lifted one whole side of the cage, and Fu crawled out. Fu stretched, and his stomach grumbled loudly. Everyone backed away, including the Governor. The Governor took the torch back and tucked the key into the folds of his robe.

"I am glad to see you've mended your pants, young man," the Governor said to Fu. "Now I wish you luck in keeping them unsoiled."

The Governor turned to the men. "Gentlemen! Please escort this poor soul to the edge of the village and let him take care of his business. Then bring him back here and lock him up. The lock will engage automatically. Simply close the cage door. I am going home to spend some time with my son. Good night."

Fu watched the Governor and Ho depart. The Governor returned the torch to its spot in front of the bun vendor's shop, and Fu saw that a large basket of rice was now sitting on the ground outside the shop's door. It could have just been an illusion from the flickering light of the torch, but the top of the basket appeared to be shaking slightly—almost like it was laughing.

"Let's go, boy," one of the men said to Fu. "We don't have all night."

Fu followed. When they reached the edge of the village, one of the men pointed to a pile of leaves beneath a large oak tree.

"There you go," the man said to Fu.

"You want me to go there?" Fu asked, surprised. "In plain sight?"

"Yes. I'm not going to let you head off into those trees alone."

Fu rubbed his bald head. He needed to think of something—fast. He closed his eyes and concentrated. A moment later, the man closest to him grabbed his nose and took several steps backward. Then the other men did the same thing, one right after another.

"Jeez, kid—that's disgusting!" one of the men said.

Fu shrugged his shoulders. "Sorry. So, who's going to follow me into the trees?"

"Nice try, monk," one of the men said. "You're NOT going into the trees. You'll go right over there where we told you to go."

Fu had no choice but to walk to the leaf pile. He walked slowly, pausing once, concentrating.

"Come on, kid!" someone blurted out. "Enough, already!"

The men backed up even more. So much more, in fact, that they were soon out of sight in the inky darkness. Fu took a deep, cleansing breath and exhaled. He wanted so badly to get down to business. However, what he wanted even more was to be free. Fu took another deep breath and ran off into the trees.

CHAPTER 25

152

"Villagers, I have returned!" Captain Yue announced the next morning. He sat atop his stallion at the edge of the village square, which was full of people. "I had to spend the night on the trail, so I'm in a terrible mood. Don't even think about trying my patience. Bring me the boy from Cangzhen Temple. NOW!"

Captain Yue was greeted with several hundred blank stares. The entire village was gathered in the square, packed tightly together around the bamboo cage. The cage door was high in the air, which meant that it was empty. Captain Yue scowled. Infuriated, he waved his hand and fifty soldiers marched up behind him, armed to the teeth. Two of the soldiers held *qiang*s. Captain Yue looked down at the two villagers who had traveled to Cangzhen to inform them of the young monk's capture.

"How dare you mock me?" Captain Yue shouted, spit flying from his flapping jaws. "You bring me here, and now your people stare at me ignorantly while standing around an empty cage? Somebody has some explaining to do. Immediately!"

Both men stared back with blank expressions. Neither of them knew what was going on, and none of the villagers wanted to tell Captain Yue that Fu had escaped.

Suddenly there was a stir among the crowd. The Governor approached Captain Yue briskly. In his hands were the dragon scrolls.

"Most honorable Captain Yue," the Governor said, bowing low. "I have what you've come for. It is with great respect I deliver these scrolls to you with my humble hands."

Captain Yue reached down from his horse and snatched all four scrolls. He opened one roughly and found it to be genuine. Then he threw it and the other three at one of his men. The soldier put the scrolls away for safekeeping.

Captain Yue stared down at the Governor. "Where is the boy?"

"I have given you the scrolls," the Governor replied simply. "Of what use is the boy?"

"You do not appear to be a fool, Governor. Do you not recall the penalty for harboring a Cangzhen monk? Bring the boy to me now, or perish."

The Governor frowned. "I'm sorry, sir. The boy has escaped."

"What?" Captain Yue shouted. "This is outrageous! How could you be so incompetent?"

"Again, I apologize," the Governor replied. "But—"

"But nothing!" Captain Yue said. "Men, string this sorry excuse for a Governor from the tallest tree. Destroy the village to teach these people a lesson!"

The soldiers rushed forward and there was a tremendous *BANG!* Everyone stopped and looked toward the source of the sound—the bamboo cage. The door had slammed shut and the lock engaged. A deep, gravelly voice spoke loudly from inside it.

"I am the one who brought trouble into this village, and I will be the one to take it out. Soldiers, take me away."

"Who is it that speaks?" Captain Yue shouted, plunging into the crowd with his horse. Several villagers cried out in pain as the heavy horse trampled upon their legs and feet, stopping only after it reached the cage. Inside sat Fu, staring defiantly up at Captain Yue.

"Who are you?" Captain Yue demanded.

"I am Fu, the one you seek. Take me, and let these good people be."

"How do I know that you are the one I seek?" Captain Yue asked.

"Because I am the one in the cage."

"The cage was empty when I arrived," Captain Yue countered. "A prisoner does not come and go as he pleases. You must be an imposter. Where is the real monk?"

"I *am* the real monk," Fu said. "I escaped last night and hid at the edge of the village. I saw you arrive and knew the Governor had promised the scrolls to you, so I decided to ambush you as you left the village. I wanted the scrolls back. But once I heard that you planned to destroy the village because I wasn't in your grasp, I decided to put myself in your hands. I don't want any more harm to come to these good people. I snuck back in here through the crowd as they all stared at you, listening to every one of your stupid words. Take me away, and leave this village alone."

The villagers stared at the cage. Every one of them was touched by Fu's words, including those villagers who wanted him gone. Only Captain Yue seemed unaffected.

"I don't believe you," Captain Yue said. "No one is that noble, especially not a child. LISTEN TO ME NOW, ONE AND ALL! I refuse to take any chances. This boy is coming with me, and so is *every* boy in this village between the ages of ten and fifteen. Hand them over immediately, or my men and I will burn this village to the ground!"

"No!" cried Fu. "You can't! *I'm* the one you want. Take me, and leave them be."

"Shut up, fat boy," Captain Yue scowled. "You're coming with me, and so are all your little friends."

"Who are you calling fat?" somebody said. Fu recognized the voice. It was the Drunkard.

"Who said that?" Captain Yue demanded.

"I did," said the heavyset Drunkard, stumbling forward as the crowd parted. He pushed his tangled hair from his eyes and stared hard at Captain Yue. "The boy may be stout, but at least he can lose some weight if he wanted to. You are a fool, and there is no cure for that."

"Watch your mouth, Drunkard," Captain Yue said. "I suggest you leave now before I let my horse trample you to pieces." The horse neighed loudly and rose up on its hind legs, pawing at the air with its deadly front hooves. Its nostrils flared savagely.

The Drunkard laughed. "You ask a horse to do your dirty work for you? I see what kind of man you are. You are weak." The Drunkard swayed from side to side, crashing heavily into the cage. If not for the stout bamboo bars, the large man would have fallen over completely.

"You try my patience, Drunkard," Captain Yue said.

"Oh, really? What does that mean? Aside from your horse, I see that you are equipped with a sword, and my ears tell me that you are also equipped with a tongue. You wield your tongue clumsily. I doubt you can do much better with your sword—or your horse."

"Ayyyaaaaa!" Captain Yue shouted as he jerked back on the reins. The horse reared up again, then came crashing down, its front legs pawing wildly at the Drunkard. For an instant, the heavyset Drunkard seemed as nimble as a cat. He darted to one side of the large, angry beast, only to stumble into the horse's side. Fu saw the Drunkard's thick right hand shoot forward to catch himself, his palm tapping the horse's rib cage before he stumbled backward. For the briefest of moments, Fu could have sworn he saw the Drunkard rooted firmly to the earth.

"Come here!" shouted Captain Yue. "You—"

The horse suddenly fell over. Captain Yue went down with it.

"ARRRR!" screamed Captain Yue as the full weight of the horse fell upon one of his long, skinny legs.

"Get this thing off me!"

Fifty soldiers rushed forward, and an entire village ran backward. An entire village, that is, except for the Drunkard, the Governor, and Ma.

CHAPTER 26

"Get out of here!" the Governor shouted at Ma, his eyes fixed on the advancing soldiers. "This is no place for you."

"Sure it is," Ma said stubbornly. "I know how to fight."

"Listen to me," the Governor said. "This is not a game. Leave, now!"

"NO!"

With the soldiers nearly upon them, the Governor did what he knew in his heart was best. He turned and kicked Ma in the backside as hard as he could, sending him flying out of harm's way. Ma sailed all the way to the outer edge of the group of villagers, and several village men grabbed him tightly to keep him from joining in the attack. Ma thrashed about violently, but found he could do nothing more than watch as the Governor ran to the cage to free Fu while the Drunkard stood his ground in front of Captain Yue and the horse. The soldiers divided into two ranks. Twenty-five men ran after the Governor. Twenty-five swarmed the Drunkard.

"Have you ever seen Drunken kung fu?" asked the Drunkard with a grin as he began to stumble around within the surging mass of soldiers. His attackers lunged inward—two and three at a time—with swords and spears. The Drunkard responded by wobbling and hobbling this way and that, bouncing unpredictably off the soldiers, one at a time. To the soldiers' complete surprise, the Drunkard's erratic movements were impossible to hit with spear or sword, and every time he stumbled into a man, that man was hurled to the ground with tremendous force. One of the soldiers even fired his *qiang* at the large, swaying target but missed cleanly. The soldiers were so occupied with trying to subdue the staggering Drunkard, none of them noticed that his seemingly random movements led the group farther and farther away from the villagers.

Unlike the Drunkard, the Governor didn't fare so well. In fact, he didn't stand a fighting chance. In the blink of an eye, he was beaten down by the second mob of ruthless soldiers and left barely conscious. A key swung loose from behind the folds of his robe, and one of the soldiers snatched it away, snapping the cord that held it. Unsure of what to do with the

Governor, the soldiers called out to Captain Yue for direction.

"I don't care about *him*!" Captain Yue shouted. "Get this stupid horse off *me*! Then get me into our sedan chair, grab the cage with the boy, and GO! We've got to get the scrolls back to Major Ying. We'll let him decide whether or not this is the right boy. Move!"

Overhearing Captain Yue's words, the Drunkard went on a major offensive. He lunged at a soldier holding a spear and removed it cleanly from the surprised man's hands. Then he started swinging. The Drunkard feinted north and struck south. He feinted east and struck west. He spun the spear before him like a windmill and soldiers dropped around him like raindrops. Fu could only see bits and pieces of the Drunkard in action, but he was impressed with what he saw. The Drunkard fought like a warrior monk. Fu thought perhaps the Drunkard really had trained at Shaolin—before he fell into the wine barrel.

Seeing the Drunkard's skill, the soldiers surrounding the cage started to hurry. Several men helped Captain Yue, while the others grabbed the cage. The cage had been lashed to two long poles along the bottom so that it could be carried like a sedan chair. The poles stretched out far beyond the front and back of the cage, which meant that the soldiers who picked Fu up were beyond his reach.

Fu flew into a rage. He threw his body first to one side of the cage, then the other in an effort to smash through the bars . . . or throw the carriers off balance . . . or something! He had to do *something*! But it was no use. The men were strong, and so was the bamboo. Defeated, Fu could only watch as he was carried to the edge of the square, toward a trail that led deep into the forest. Fu let out a desperate cry. And for once, someone listened.

The Drunkard looked up, his eyes locking on Fu's. Something stirred deep in Fu's heart. Fu froze, paralyzed by a feeling he had never known. The Drunkard froze, too. Something powerful passed between them and the Drunkard roared. Fu saw a soldier grab hold of the Drunkard's tattered robe, and with one mighty swipe, the Drunkard crushed the man's shoulder. The Drunkard leaped toward Fu, leaving just one soldier standing. A soldier with a *qiang*.

Across the square, Ma tensed in the arms of the village men still holding him back. As the soldier raised the *qiang*, Ma squatted into a Horse Stance and lashed out with his right leg, striking one of his captors square in the knee. The village man cried out and released his grip on Ma. Ma tore free of the other two sets of hands and raced across the square, screaming at the top of his lungs.

The soldier with the *qiang* hesitated. He looked at the wild boy racing toward him, then looked at the Drunkard racing away from him. He lined the *qiang* up with the center of the Drunkard's back and pulled the trigger.

There was a slight pause before the gunpowder ignited. It was during this pause that Ma smashed into the soldier. The end of the *qiang* swung downward, and the powder exploded. Five steps from the cage, the Drunkard cried out, stumbling forward. He reached out toward Fu, then fell to the ground.

Fu watched helplessly as his cage was swallowed by the overgrown trail.

CHAPTER
27

Fu swayed from side to side as the caravan of soldiers pushed forward on the narrow trail. It was the middle of the day, but Fu's world was dark. Captain Yue had ordered his men to cover Fu's cage with several blankets, like a shade for a birdcage. At the head of the caravan, Captain Yue sat high in a sedan chair behind a shade of his own. His, however, was made of silk. As Captain Yue and Fu rode along behind their separate shrouds, they both thought about the exact same thing: pain. The pain Captain Yue felt seeped from the outside in as a result of the injury to his leg. Fu's, however, oozed from the inside out. Out from someplace deep down in his heart.

Fu was alone. More alone than he had ever been in

his entire life. The look in the Drunkard's eyes had shown him that. Their connection was brief, but powerful. In that instant, Fu knew the Drunkard cared for him. Deeply. He could feel it. He didn't question it. But he did question why the Drunkard felt that way. The Drunkard was a complete stranger, yet he had risked his life for him. In fact, he may have even *lost* his life for him. Fu had heard the Drunkard cry out and seen him fall. The way Fu's luck worked, the Drunkard was probably dead. It would only make sense. Fu had already been abandoned by everyone else in his life. Why not the Drunkard, too?

Fu sighed. The tiger cub had left him and so had his brothers. True, Grandmaster had told him and his brothers to separate and run, but his brothers didn't have to do it. They could have stayed and done something. He did. He would have been more successful if he had had some help. But, instead, they had left him to do it all himself. Alone.

The cage suddenly jerked to a stop, and Fu bumped his bald head against the bamboo bars.

"Stupid—" Fu began to say.

"HALT!" a stranger's voice commanded from somewhere up the trail. "Who goes there?"

Captain Yue cleared his throat. "It is I—Captain Yue of Major Ying's army!" he announced. "Who dares to stand on the trail before my caravan, commanding me to halt?"

The stranger up the trail laughed. "Who am I? I am Commander Woo, you arrogant snob. If you would stick your pointed head out from behind your precious silk curtains and take a look, you would see for yourself."

Fu found a seam where two blankets overlapped and peeked out. He saw a bend in the trail ahead. On it was a second caravan headed straight toward their caravan. A stocky man clad in armor stood at the head of the second caravan, glaring at Captain Yue's sedan chair. Fu assumed he was Commander Woo.

Fu saw Captain Yue stick his head out from behind the silk curtains.

"Oh, so it *is* you," Captain Yue said to Commander Woo.

Commander Woo looked around. "Where is your horse? Have you given him away so that you can travel like a princess? Be a man for once in your life. Get down here and walk with your troops."

"I can't walk, you ignorant oaf," Captain Yue replied. "I've been injured and so has my horse, not that it's any of your business. Where is Major Ying?"

"Excuse me?" Commander Woo said. He stepped forward and his eyes narrowed. "The Emperor may be your uncle, Captain Yue, but that doesn't give you the right to talk back to me that way. I am your superior. Never forget that."

"Sorry, *sir*," Captain Yue said. He closed his eyes. "Commander, could you *please* tell me where Major Ying is?"

"Major Ying had some business to attend to, so he sent me and these men to rendezvous with you. Were you successful in obtaining the scrolls and the young monk?"

"Of course," Captain Yue replied.

"Then hand them over."

"Nothing would please me more than to be done with this nonsense," Captain Yue said. "My own number one man has the scrolls. He will retrieve them now. As soon as they are in your hands, I shall be on my way. I must seek treatment immediately."

Commander Woo snorted. "You will go nowhere until I say so, Princess."

A moment later, Fu saw one of Captain Yue's men appear with all four scrolls. The soldier handed them over to Commander Woo.

"Would you like to see the boy in the cage?" Captain Yue asked. He yanked his curtains open and leaned back.

"Not just yet," Commander Woo replied. "I want to check the scrolls first."

"I can assure you, they're authentic," Captain Yue said.

"I'll be the judge of that."

Commander Woo opened one of the scrolls, and Fu saw his tiny eyes widen. He handed the three remaining scrolls over to a skinny man and instructed the man to follow. The scroll-bearer put the three scrolls into the folds of his robe. Fu watched both men leave the narrow trail and walk over to a small clearing.

Fu shook his head. Who did this Commander

Woo think he was? Cangzhen monks had to prove themselves elite before they were allowed to view the secret scrolls for their style. Fu could tell simply by the way this man walked he had not studied kung fu very long. His stumpy torso and short legs wobbled in opposition as he ambled toward the clearing. Commander Woo may be powerful and know how to fight other soldiers in combat situations, but kung fu was another story altogether. Especially the advanced kung fu found in the scrolls. Worst of all, the Commander's body style was completely inappropriate for most dragon-style techniques. Things were about to get ugly. Very ugly.

Commander Woo assumed a sloppy Horse Stance and adjusted the flexible armor draped over his wide torso. He handed the remaining scroll to the scroll-bearer.

"Hold this scroll open in front of you for a moment," Commander Woo said. "I want to try something."

From the awkward, shoulder-width Horse Stance, Commander Woo kept his right foot rooted and stepped backward with his left. After shifting his center of gravity, he leaned forward with his upper body and formed dragon claws with both hands by extending his fingers, separating them, and bending only his fingertips at the first knuckle. He put his left claw slightly in front of the right, overlapping at the thumbs. Then he positioned both claws up near his face and brought his elbows in. He compressed every muscle in his body, as if bracing for an impact. Though his form was poor, Fu recognized this as a classic defensive dragon position.

What is he going to do from here? Fu wondered.

Without additional preparation or adjustments, Commander Woo suddenly whipped his back leg around at waist height. His leg was bent, and as it neared the front of his body, he straightened it, snapping it powerfully as though it were a dragon's tail. Fu and the others heard a tremendous *POP!*, and the powerful man pretending to be a dragon fell to the ground, howling in pain. The scroll-bearer ran to his side, tucking the open scroll into the folds of his robe along with the other three. He helped Commander Woo up.

The Commander clamped his jaws shut and bit down hard, grunting loudly as he rested all his weight on his left leg—the one that had swung like a dragon's tail. It held his weight just fine. Then he attempted to lift his right leg—the one that had been firmly rooted. He managed to raise his thigh up parallel to the ground, but nothing else attached to that leg responded. Everything below the knee dangled like a tired fish flopping at the end of a silk fishing line. Commander Woo howled again.

As if in response, a tremendous screeching suddenly filled the air around them.

"ON YOUR GUARD!" one of the soldiers shouted. "MONKEY TROOP! PROTECT THE SUPPLY CARTS!"

Chapter 28

One hundred brown macaques descended upon the caravan from the treetops. Fu had never seen anything like it. The medium-size monkeys tore into everything in sight, each one scrambling to find something edible to steal as the soldiers attempted to beat them off with spears. The monkeys' quick, erratic movements were too unpredictable. The soldiers were spectacularly unsuccessful.

A man shrieked, and Fu looked over to see Captain Yue slapping at a small monkey. The monkey ran off, and Captain Yue tied his silk curtains closed. Fu scanned the area and found Commander Woo hobbling over to one of the weapons carts, using the skinny scroll-bearer as a crutch. The skinny man helped Commander Woo clear out a space and climb into the cart. Then he closed a wooden hatch, securing Commander Woo inside. The skinny man grabbed a spear, and Fu watched as the man tried with great frustration to run the spear through a monkey or two. The man wielded the weapon poorly. He would make an easy target if Fu ever got out.

As Fu continued to watch the skinny soldier, something landed on top of his cage. From the sound, Fu assumed it was one of the larger monkeys.

"Stupid monkey!" Fu shouted. "You won't find any food in here!"

The monkey stopped moving. It suddenly leaped, screeching loudly, and came down heavily on the cage directly above Fu. Its foot landed between two of the bamboo bars and crashed down on top of Fu's head, covered by the blanket. Fu grabbed the foot through the blanket and yanked hard. The creature squealed. As Fu hung on, deciding what to do next, his nose recoiled. He knew that smell!

"Malao, it's me! Fu! Get me out of here!"

Malao jerked his foot up and the blanket went with it. He stuck his small, smiling face down between two bamboo bars running across the top of the cage. Beads of sweat dripped off his bald, dark-skinned head.

"Pussycat!" Malao said, giggling. "How did you get in there?"

"How did I get in here?" Fu said. "What are you doing up there?"

"I was—"

Malao disappeared. A soldier had grabbed his ankle and yanked him off the cage.

"Malao!" Fu cried as he found a seam between more blankets on the far side of the cage. He looked out and saw Malao twist and wiggle and kick and claw and bite, all at the same time. The soldier trying to hold on to him threw his hands up in the air and stepped back. Malao hit the ground and let out a shriek, leaping back up on top of Fu's cage. He tore the remaining blankets off and began to beat his chest like an angry ape, sending a piercing scream in the direction of the soldiers. The soldiers stopped and stared. Fu stared, too. He had never seen Malao like this before.

As Malao carried on, Fu slammed his hand against the top of the cage. "Hey, Monkey Boy! Remember me? Get me out of here!"

"Out! Out! Out!" Malao screeched as he jumped up and down atop the cage like one of the macaques, all the while slyly scanning the soldiers. A key ring glimmered in a soldier's hand, and Malao leaped at the man without hesitation. Soaring feetfirst through the air, Malao arrived with one leg on either side of the soldier's long neck. He locked his ankles behind the man's head and squeezed, scissor-style, while twisting his body to one side. The soldier folded in half sideways and choked, releasing the keys so that he could grab Malao's legs. The keys hit the ground the same time Malao did. Malao scrambled off the shaken man and grabbed the key ring. Five men sprang on him at once.

Malao managed to throw the key ring between the men an instant before he was pounded into the earth. The keys sailed through the bars of the cage, right into Fu's lap. Fu began fumbling through keys as Malao got pummeled. In no time, Fu found a key that looked about right and reached his arm through the bars to try it in the lock. Out of the corner of his eye, he saw a soldier running toward him with a spear.

Fu pretended not to see the soldier and didn't flinch until the moment the soldier thrust his spear. Fu dropped the keys and twisted gracefully to his left side, lifting his right arm high as the spear tip breezed underneath his armpit. As the soldier withdrew the spear, Fu bent his right elbow and clamped it down as hard as he could on top of the spear shaft. Then he gripped the shaft with his right hand and jerked his body powerfully backward. The soldier was not rooted and lurched forward with the spear, smashing his head against the bamboo bars. Fu lunged forward himself, grabbing the man's long black hair with one hand between the bars. Fu shoved straight down as hard as he could. There was a sharp crack as the soldier's nose shattered against a large stone. Still conscious, the man ripped his head away from Fu and screamed as a fistful of his hair remained in Fu's hand. A chunk of scalp dangled from the clump of hair. Fu dropped it in the dirt and stared hard at the man. The man grabbed the hairy clump and ran away. Fu got back to work.

Fu grabbed the keys, unlocked the latch, and threw the door up. Then he grabbed the spear the soldier had left behind and headed for Malao. But after only two steps, he stopped dead in his tracks. He couldn't believe his eyes. Monkeys were pouring out of the trees, leaping directly onto the heads, backs, arms, and legs of the soldiers on top of Malao. In no time, there was an undulating pile of more than fifty monkeys, clawing, scratching, and biting in unison. The men cried out in pain as more and more monkeys joined the savage attack, all of them abandoning their previous scavenging in the food carts in order to help Malao.

Fu had no idea what was going on, but he wasn't about to get close enough to that pile to find out. Instead, he looked for the skinny soldier with the scrolls and spotted the man standing next to one of the supply carts staring open-mouthed at the monkey pile. Fu ran directly for him.

The soldier saw Fu coming and did his best to brace himself for the attack. He assumed a defensive position with his spear held before him, holding his ground as Fu started swinging. Fu feinted high and swung low with his own spear, bringing one end around behind the soldier's knees. The soldier's legs buckled forward, and before he even hit the ground, Fu swiftly pulled the spear back and swung it up over his head and down, as though he were chopping wood with an ax. The spear shaft connected with the soldier's unprotected collarbone.

The spear was strong. The collarbone was not.

The soldier bellowed in pain as he crumpled to his knees. Fu slid one hand up his spear's shaft so that his hands were shoulder-width apart, then lunged forward with the spear before him, parallel to the ground. The shaft connected with the soldier's windpipe, and Fu leaned into it. The soldier toppled over backward as Fu hopped on top of the spear shaft, placing one knee on either side of the soldier's head, pinning the soldier to the ground by his throat. The soldier gasped for air. He was unsuccessful. As soon as the man was unconscious, Fu let up on the spear, spun around, and retrieved all four scrolls from the folds of the soldier's robe.

As he stood, Fu realized something. None of the remaining soldiers had come to aid the scroll-bearer. He looked around and saw that the screeching monkeys were now chasing all the soldiers off into the forest. Fu looked over at Malao and once again could hardly believe his own eyes.

Malao stood firm and straight as blood poured heavily out of both sides of his nose. He pointed at the fleeing soldiers with his arms outstretched, and the monkey troop pursued as if following orders. The five soldiers who had attacked Malao lay at his feet, their bodies scratched and clawed and broken. A large, snow-white, one-eyed monkey sat on Malao's shoulder.

Malao smiled at Fu and laughed out loud as he

lowered his arms and relaxed. The monkey seemed to laugh, too. Then it leaned forward as if to kiss Malao's bald head and scampered off into the trees.

CHAPTER 29

"**W**hat was THAT all about?" Fu asked Malao, bewildered.

Malao casually leaned his small head back and pinched the bridge of his nose to slow the flow of blood out of his nostrils. "What was what?"

"The white monkey!" Fu said. "All the monkeys!"

"It's a long story," Malao replied, shrugging his shoulders. "A *really* long story."

Fu growled. He took a step toward Malao, then stopped suddenly and looked suspiciously up into the trees behind Malao. Malao giggled.

"Don't be a scaredy-cat," Malao said. "You can approach me."

"I'm not afraid," Fu snapped. "I'm just . . . confused.

Did you command those monkeys to attack?"

"What did it look like?" Malao asked, flashing a devilish grin.

"I'm not in the mood for riddles," Fu said. "If you're not going to answer my questions, just say so."

Malao pouted. "Come on, Pussycat. Humor me. I save your life, and this is how you treat me?"

"You know how much I hate your games, Malao. I appreciate your saving me and all, but I'm really not in the mood. I don't want to get angry at you."

"You appreciate me?" Malao said, grinning wide. He put his hand on his heart. "Really? Brother Fu, I'm touched!"

Fu growled again. "Don't push me, Monkey Brains."

"*That's* the Fu I know!" Malao exclaimed. "Welcome back!"

Fu closed his eyes and ground his teeth. "The Fu you know will never be back. I left him at Cangzhen."

"Whoa, what's with all the drama?" Malao said. "Those villagers must have really worked you over."

Fu opened his eyes and cocked his head to one side. "How do you know about the villagers?"

"A little bird told me." Malao smiled.

"Stop screwing around, Malao."

"What!" Malao said, stomping his foot. "I'm talking about Hok!"

"Hok?" Fu said, surprised. "When did you see Hok?"

"I don't know. You know how easily I forget things. I just remember that I saw him a couple of times after you ran away from Cangzhen."

"Ran away!" Fu said in disbelief. "I didn't run away. You guys did. *I* stayed and fought. *I* got the scrolls. You guys left me to fight, alone."

"Not exactly," Malao replied. "We all ran like Grandmaster said, but Hok and I circled back separately. I was just heading to the village now to help you. My new friends were showing me the way when they got hungry and decided to raid the caravan. I had no idea you were in the cage until I heard your voice."

Fu didn't know what to say. He looked over at Malao, speechless. Malao seemed to read the look in Fu's eyes.

"You're welcome, Pussycat," he said.

Fu lowered his eyes and shuffled his feet.

Malao scratched his small, bald head. "Hey, are those the dragon scrolls?"

Fu saw that one of the scrolls was poking out of his robe. "Yeah," he said. "I have all four."

"How did you get ahold of them?"

"It's a long story," Fu replied. "A *really* long story."

Malao laughed out loud. "That's pretty funny! Good one, Fu! Can I see one of those scrolls for a moment? I've always wondered what they look like."

"Sure," Fu said. "Just make sure you—"

As Fu reached into his robe, he heard a *whoosh!* and a quick *clink!-clink!-clink!* Malao's face hit the dirt as his feet were jerked out from under him by a chain whip.

Chapter 30

'79

"Come here, you little knuckle-dragger!" Ying snarled as he stepped out of a thick bush behind Malao, holding the chain whip. The deep grooves in his face seemed to slither under the strain as he began pulling Malao toward him, hand over hand. Several paces away, Fu was about to make a move when a battalion of well-armed soldiers appeared on the trail. Leading the group was a man with a long ponytail braid riding a raven-black stallion. Fu recognized the man immediately. Directly behind the horse, two men each carried one end of a long pole with something orange strung to it, hanging down, swaying as they walked. The swaying object was Hok. His pale wrists were bound together, and so were his ankles. The long pole passed beneath the bindings, and Hok hung from it like a hunting trophy. Fu paused to take it all in until Malao's cries brought him back to the moment.

"FU! HELP ME!"

With one great bound, Fu was at Malao's wriggling feet. He reached down and grabbed the chain whip, entering into a tug-of-war with Ying.

A series of piercing shrieks suddenly rang out from the treetops, and Fu turned to see the white monkey leading dozens of brown macaques toward Ying.

"FIRE!" Ying commanded, still holding fast to the chain whip. The soldiers raised their *qiang*s and shots rang out. Monkeys tumbled from the sky. A lead ball grazed the arm of the white monkey, and it screeched loudly, turning tail. The rest of the monkeys followed its retreat.

Ying laughed. "Fine fighting force you have there, Malao."

"Finer than the men you lost at Cangzhen!" Fu growled as he continued to heave on the chain while Malao struggled to get free. "At least most of the monkeys . . . *GRRRRR* . . . escaped . . . *ARRRRR* . . . alive!"

Fu gave a tremendous jerk to try and get Malao a little more slack. Ying let go. Fu sailed backward, the chain whip slipping from his grasp. Ying leaped forward with his arms spread wide. He landed directly on top of Malao.

"Don't let him grab you!" Fu cried out to Malao.

But it was too late. Ying already had a crippling eagle-claw grip sinking deep into a pressure point on Malao's neck. Malao's entire body went limp. Lines of blood trickled down toward his shoulder as Ying's long fingernails dug in. Fu knew that he had to break that grip, or Malao would suffer permanent nerve damage.

Fu ran full-force into Ying's arm, breaking Ying's connection with Malao. Ying responded by latching on to the back of Fu's neck with his other hand with amazing speed. This time, it was Fu who went limp. Malao, still temporarily paralyzed, lay motionless. Ying lessened his grip on Fu slightly and removed the scrolls from Fu's robe with his free hand as he addressed his men.

"Did all of you see that? That is how you take care of business! Quickly, efficiently, decisively!"

Ying turned to Commander Woo, who sat in the weapons cart with the hatch open.

"COMMANDER WOO!" Ying said, pointing to Hok hanging from the pole. "Look what Tonglong has caught. There is your restless spirit from Cangzhen, hanging from that pole. He was the one you felt watching you, and he snatched the Grandmaster's body from beneath your nose. Hobble over there on your one good leg and untie the one called Hok so that he can walk. He's going on a little trip.

"CAPTAIN YUE! Get yourself out from behind those curtains this instant." Captain Yue poked his head out. Ying continued. "You will tie up the two troublemakers known as Fu and Malao, and they, too, will walk. Their paralysis is only temporary, so I suggest you hurry.

"TONGLONG! You have proven your loyalty to me by capturing Hok. Now it is time for you to get your hands dirty. You will finish what was left unfinished back at the temple. Kill these monks. We'll set up camp here for the night, so make sure you take them far into the forest before completing the job. I don't want any tigers coming around here to dine on their corpses or lap up their blood. If you run into any problems, fire a warning shot from a *qiang*. I'd hate to have to interrupt my reading to clean up any mess you might make, so don't make any mistakes. And make sure you pay special attention to Fu. He's already gotten away from you once."

"I give you my word," Tonglong said with a gleam in his eye. "I'll take care of the one called Fu."

Fu stumbled sluggishly forward as Tonglong pushed him from behind. He nearly fell several times because his legs didn't respond as quickly as they normally did thanks to Ying temporarily interrupting the natural flow of energy through his nervous system. Malao appeared to be in a little better shape, moving forward behind Tonglong while two soldiers pushed him along. Bringing up the rear, two more soldiers followed Hok.

Fu considered their odds. There were four soldiers plus Tonglong against him and two of his brothers. Two of the soldiers carried spears and one carried a *qiang*, while each warrior monk was tightly bound with rope from shoulder to waist, their arms pinned to their sides and their ankles connected by a short length of rope. He and his brothers didn't stand a chance. Fu figured Tonglong would finish him first, especially after their encounter back at Cangzhen.

Fu slowed for a moment to steady himself as they entered a sun-drenched clearing. He squinted and coughed quietly to clear his dry throat. Tonglong stepped up to him and screamed in his face.

"What did you just say?"

"Nothing," Fu replied. "I didn't say—"

"Don't deny it!" Tonglong shouted, pushing Fu to the edge of the clearing. He pulled his long, thick braid forward over his shoulder and tucked it into his sash. "You mumbled a secret under that cough. Who is listening on the wind, one of your remaining brothers? Let us find him before he attacks us! You will be my shield."

Tonglong shoved Fu hard into an enormous bush. Fu was swallowed whole. The soldiers guarding Hok and Malao looked about warily as Tonglong leaped into the bush after Fu. He, too, disappeared completely. Fu lay on the ground, confused, as Tonglong landed on top of him and spoke in whispers.

"I realize none of your remaining brothers are near, young monk. I simply said that as an excuse to get you alone for a moment. I still owe you a life. I am loosening your bonds as I speak. When we get back out in the open, you must pretend to attack me so that I will not lose face."

"But—"

"Hush!" Tonglong said. "Do not speak. Do you practice Iron Head kung fu?"

Fu nodded.

"Good. I will carry you out into the open and pretend to crush your rib cage with my Iron Arms. Use your Iron Head skills to strike my head just hard enough to render me unconscious. There is a dagger in my sash. Use it to cut your brothers free, but I ask that you leave it behind. It is important to me. You must not take my sword, either. Agreed?"

Fu thought for a moment. Didn't this man know that he had already returned the favor? He had saved his life back at Cangzhen when he distracted Ying by yelling from the burning rooftop after Ying killed Grandmaster.

Tonglong grunted impatiently. Fu nodded in agreement. Without warning, Tonglong slapped him loudly on the side of his bald head. It was a glancing blow, but it still hurt.

"Take that!" Tonglong screamed at Fu. "Don't you dare try to sneak away from me! Now stand up so I can knock you down again!"

Fu stood as best he could amid the dense foliage, irritated by the sharp slap. Tonglong gripped him chest to chest in a tight bear hug and carried him a few steps out into the open, squeezing harder than Fu thought necessary. Fu grunted. If this man wanted to see a little Iron Head technique, then that's exactly what he would get. Fu snapped his head back and then forward with lightning speed. Tonglong looked surprised as Fu's forehead met his left temple. Tonglong slid to the ground, his eyes closed. Fu stepped back and wiggled slightly. The ropes dropped to his feet.

Seeing Fu in action, Malao lunged at the nearest soldier, swinging his head.

The soldier put his hands in front of his face to protect himself, and his fingers were crushed between Malao's iron-like forehead and his own forehead. The soldier dropped to his knees, his crumpled fingers held out before him. He stared hard at Malao with fight in his eyes.

Malao leaped straight into the air, his ankles tied together with a length of rope about half as long as his arm. He tucked into a tight forward flip just as the soldier began to stand and completed his improvised maneuver by thrusting his legs forward, spreading them out as far as the rope would allow, and slamming the taut rope down against the back of the soldier's neck. The soldier's head snapped down and his torso followed, his body going limp after his face ricocheted off a fallen tree. Malao tucked his chin to his chest as his upper back hit the ground smoothly. He rocked forward, popping up onto his feet. Then he turned to face the second soldier who had been guarding him.

The second soldier carried a *qiang*. Malao stopped his attack. Fu, however, did not. He had retrieved the dagger from Tonglong's sash and was about to throw it at the soldier when the soldier suddenly turned the *qiang* toward Fu.

"Put the dagger down, monk," the soldier said. "Now."

Fu hesitated. He glanced across the clearing and saw that the two soldiers guarding Hok had knocked him to the ground. They stood over Hok with their spears raised, ready to thrust. Malao stood uninjured, but he was securely bound and quite some distance from everyone else.

"Drop the dagger," the soldier with the *qiang* repeated. "I will count to three."

Fu stood there, thinking.

"One . . . two . . ."

Suddenly there was a loud *CRASH!* as something exploded from the brush behind the soldier. Startled, Fu looked toward the sound, expecting to see a white monkey flying through the air. Instead, a large tiger cub slammed into the soldier with the *qiang*. The cub's front claws sunk deep into the soldier's shoulder blades, and the man fell forward, screaming. The cub raked at the man's back ferociously, all the while staring at Fu.

Wide-eyed, one of the soldiers standing over Hok shouted, "Look! That tiger is protecting the large monk! Just like the monkeys fought for the small monk earlier!"

"You're right!" the other soldier replied. "I'm not going to lay a hand on any of them! Let's get out of here!"

Both men ran, and the tiger cub jerked its head in their direction. Then it turned back toward Fu and blinked three times before instinctively giving chase. The cub left his victim in a state of shock, lying flat on his stomach with his arms outstretched.

Malao and Hok stared at Fu. Fu stared back. He shrugged his shoulders and a small drop of blood fell from the corner of the cut across his cheek.

"**W**hat was THAT all about!" Malao shrieked excitedly as he hobbled over to Fu, his arms and legs tied.

"Oh," Fu said casually as he wiped the drop of blood with his thumb and popped it into his mouth. "It's a *really* long story."

Malao giggled. "Good one, Fu!"

"I can't wait to hear it," said Hok as he approached, still bound.

"You can't wait to hear my story?" Fu said to Hok. "What about your story? Never before have I seen a crane hanging from a trophy pole like a deer!"

"I suppose I do have a story or two to share," Hok said. "But not right now. Would you be so kind as to cut us loose? We need to leave as soon as possible."

"I'll cut you guys loose," Fu said as he went to work on Hok's ropes, "but I'm not going anywhere. Not without those scrolls."

Hok shook his head. "It's not worth it, Fu. Ying is too strong."

Fu stopped cutting and glared at Hok. "What do you suggest we do instead, run away? Look where that got you."

"Hey, hey, hey!" Malao interrupted. "Be nice, Fu."

Fu grunted and got back to work.

Malao watched Fu cut Hok's ropes. "How did you get free, Fu? I mean, one moment you're tied up like me and Hok, and the next you're not. What happened in that bush with Tonglong?"

"Who?" Fu asked.

"Tonglong," Malao replied. "You know, Ying's number one soldier? The man with the long ponytail?"

"Is that his name?" Fu asked. "'Praying mantis'? What kind of name is that?"

"I don't know," Hok replied. "Cantonese, I suppose."

"No kidding," Fu said. He finished with Hok and walked over to Malao. He started cutting and said, "I spared Tonglong's life back at Cangzhen, and he repaid the debt. That's all. He let me loose, and now we're even. If he ever stands between me and the scrolls, he'll taste my fist!"

"Let it go, Fu," Hok said, rubbing his pale, chafed

wrists. "Ying and Tonglong are far too strong. You won't have a chance."

"I have to get the scrolls back!" Fu said, holding up Tonglong's dagger. "I refuse to let Ying win."

"Just let it go," Hok repeated. "I'm telling you, Ying's reach is too great. He has information, and information is power."

"What do you mean by that?" Fu asked.

Hok sighed. "I overheard Ying talking to Tonglong. It seems Ying has been very busy this past year. Not only has he joined the Emperor, trained troops, and risen quickly through the ranks, he's also done quite a bit of research into his own past. I heard some of the stories he shared with Tonglong, and they seem believable to me."

Fu finished freeing Malao. He looked at Hok. "Back at Cangzhen, Ying told me that Grandmaster wasn't the holy man everyone thinks he was. Is that what you're talking about?"

"Possibly," Hok said. "Ying told Tonglong that Cangzhen Temple was a base for secret activities, and that we warrior monks were nothing but security guards whose main role was to protect Grandmaster and help with his secret operations."

"That's crazy," Fu said.

"I thought so, too," Hok replied. "At first."

"At first? Ying is just making up stories to justify attacking Cangzhen."

"That was my first reaction. But now I'm not so sure. Grandmaster kept a lot of things from us, you know."

"Like what?" Fu asked.

"For instance," Hok said. "Grandmaster had visitors on occasion. What kind of *secret* temple has visitors?"

"You're paranoid."

"Really?" Hok asked. "Why did our temple have to be secret in the first place? Think about it, Fu. Also, we all know that Grandmaster wasn't raised at Cangzhen like us, right? He led a different life before coming to Cangzhen, and like so many other things, his previous life was kept secret from us."

"I think we need more information before we pass judgment on Grandmaster," Fu said.

"Look at you, Governor Fu!" Malao said with a laugh. "Since when did you become so diplomatic?"

"Be quiet, Malao," Fu growled. "Hok and I haven't finished our conversation."

"You two *never* finish conversations when you get into this kind of mood," Malao said. "You're both way too hardheaded. Only you could make a crane talk so much, Fu."

Fu growled again. Malao giggled.

Hok closed his eyes. "We'll be finished in a few moments, Malao. I only have a few more things to say." He opened his eyes and looked at Fu. "I agree that we still need more information before we pass judgment. At the same time, I think you should give Ying's story some thought. Ying is many things to many people, but I've never known him to be a liar."

"He *is* a liar!" Fu roared. "A liar, a thief, and a

murderer! How can you defend Ying like this? He is responsible for the deaths of our brothers and the destruction of our home!"

"I'm not defending Ying's actions," Hok said. "I'm only sharing information with you. There is something else you should know. Something important. We know that Ying destroyed our temple and killed our brothers because of his hatred toward Grandmaster. I assumed his hatred stemmed from the death of his best friend and our dear brother Luk last year, but it seems that was only part of it. Ying also believes that his own father was killed by Grandmaster."

"What?" Fu said. "That's nonsense."

"Fu, listen carefully," Hok said. "According to Ying, Grandmaster killed his father in order to steal the secret dragon scrolls. All we really know about Grandmaster is that he came to Cangzhen with amazing, never-before-seen dragon kung fu techniques. Those techniques came from those scrolls, and those scrolls are ancient. Grandmaster did not write them himself. They had to come from somewhere. And if Ying's father was a dragon-style master, it would explain why Ying has always yearned to be a dragon himself."

"This is crazy," Fu said.

"I know it sounds crazy," Hok said. "But it could very well be true."

"I still don't believe it. Not if it came from Ying's forked tongue."

"Would you believe someone else?" Hok asked.

"Perhaps," Fu said. "But who is left alive that could tell us more about Cangzhen's history?"

"I've been thinking a lot about that question," Hok replied, "because I want to believe that Ying's claims are false. I think perhaps the monks at Shaolin could help. After all, Cangzhen was founded by Shaolin monks."

"That's a great idea!" Malao said. "I've always wanted to go to Shaolin!"

"It seems like a good idea to me, too," Fu said. "I just met someone who may have trained at Shaolin, and I'd like to find out more about him. But first I need to get the scrolls back. I'm not going anywhere without them. I'm serious."

"Is it really worth it, Fu?" Hok asked. "Ying is more powerful than you know. You should let it go."

"We could do it if we worked together," Fu said, slamming his fist into his open palm. "I know we could."

"Trust me, Fu," Hok said. "We can't succeed. If we had Seh and Long with us, we might stand a chance, but Malao has discovered that Seh is off recruiting additional helpers, and Long has disappeared without a trace. I don't think you realize what we're up against. Ying has grown stronger since he left Cangzhen, and Tonglong is unbelievable. Tonglong's hearing and eyesight are amazing, and his kung fu is very powerful—different from anything I've ever seen before. He's the one who caught me."

"I defeated him once," Fu said. "I can do it again."

"I mean you no disrespect, Fu," said Hok, "but I think perhaps you got lucky."

"Oh, yeah? Well, I think—"

"Stop it!" Malao shouted. "Stop it right now! You are the two most stubborn people I've ever met in my life! We need to get going!"

"I'm not going anywhere," Fu said. "Not without the scrolls."

Malao rolled his eyes. He looked at Hok. "What are you going to do?"

Hok took a deep breath. "I've decided that I'm going to Shaolin. Alone, if I have to."

Fu looked at Malao. "I guess it's up to you."

Malao blinked. "Me? Why *me*? You know I can't make decisions."

"Just pick one," Fu said. "I'm staying. He's going. It's that simple."

Malao shuffled his feet.

"Pick one, Malao," Fu urged. "Him? Or me?"

"Or you can go off alone," Hok added.

Malao twitched. "Alone? I don't want to be alone. . . ."

Fu froze. He locked eyes with Malao and something powerful passed between them. Fu realized he and Malao had something in common after all. Just like true brothers.

Malao smiled at Fu. "I think I'll—"

KAA-BOOM!

The three young warrior monks jumped. Fu

looked over at the soldier who had been attacked by the cub and saw the man still lying on his stomach. The soldier's smoking *qiang* lay just within his reach, his limp hand on the trigger. Fu saw a splintered hole at the base of a tree next to the soldier. The soldier had successfully fired a warning shot.

Fu turned back to Malao.

Malao smiled again. "Let's have some fun, Pussy-cat!"

And for the first time since Ying returned to Cangzhen, Fu smiled.

Lying at the foot of a large bush, his face pressed deep in the dirt, Tonglong also smiled.

ACKNOWLEDGMENTS

First and foremost, I must thank my amazing agent, Laura Rennert, for both her editorial guidance and business acumen, and my remarkable editors, Jim Thomas and Schuyler Hooke—two great guys who changed my writing forever.

It's also important for me to thank Andrea Brown and Magnus Toren for putting together the annual Big Sur Children's Writing Workshop. Without Big Sur, this series wouldn't exist. And without Big Sur, I would never have met Susan Hart Lindquist and Amanda Conran, who've both had a major impact on my writing (though I think only one of them knows it). Nancy Lamb has also made a big difference through our friendship formed at Big Sur and her fantastic book on crafting stories for children.

Another author-friend, Kelly James-Enger, deserves a big thank-you for her huge amounts of maniac support and tarot card readings, and someone at the Carmel Clay Public Library deserves a big thank-you for designing a spectacular building with numerous nooks and study rooms where an aspiring author can write.

I can't forget to thank my kung fu instructor, John Vaughn of Shaolin-Do, for being a phenomenal teacher and all-around nice guy.

Family is important to me, and I have to thank my parents, Roger and Arlene, as well as my brothers, Joe and Jaysen, for giving me their all when I was young and for always being there whenever I stop to make time for them now that I've more or less grown up.

Finally, my wife Jeanie, daughter Tristen, and son Owen get the biggest thank-you of all for their love and support as I continue to chase the Five Ancestors, along with my dreams. You guys are the best!

The adventure continues
with the second of
THE FIVE ANCESTORS . . .
MONKEY!

Prologue

For the first time in a thousand years, there was thunder in the temple.

Hidden inside the heavy terracotta barrel at the back of the practice hall, eleven-year-old Malao flinched with every BOOM, every CRACK! Thunder inside their compound could only come from one source. A dragon. A very angry dragon.

Malao shivered. According to legend, dragons controlled the wind and the rain, the lightning and the thunder. Stay in a dragon's good graces, and your crops would receive enough rain for a bountiful harvest; anger a dragon, and your crops would be washed away—along with you, your house, and your entire family. Push a dragon too far, and it would deliver a special kind of storm, smashing everything it could with its powerful tail, igniting everything that remained with its fiery breath.

A dragon must be the reason Grandmaster had made Malao and his four "temple" brothers—Fu, Seh, Hok, and Long—squeeze into the barrel. Grandmaster had told them they were under attack by soldiers, but Malao knew men alone could never defeat the warrior monks of Cangzhen Temple. The attackers must have formed an alliance with a dragon. What could those thunderclaps be but the crack of a dragon snapping its enormous tail?

A dragon lashing its tail reminded Malao of his older brother Ying and his chain whip. Ying had left Cangzhen in a rage the year before, upset because he had been trained his entire life as an eagle but had always wanted to be an all-powerful dragon. Swinging his chain whip was the closest Ying had ever come to having a dragon tail of his own.

Malao shivered again. Ying had vowed to return to Cangzhen to punish Grandmaster for training him as an eagle, but Ying was no fool. He would never attack Cangzhen and its one hundred warrior monks unless he was guaranteed victory. And for that to happen, he would have to have had acquired power beyond that of mortal men—

"Oh, no!" Malao thought. "Maybe Ying has figured out a way to transform himself into a real dragon! Maybe he has grown scales and a tail and—"

KA-BOOM!

Jeff Stone lives in the Midwest with his wife and two children and practices the martial arts daily. He has worked as a photographer, an editor, a maintenance man, a technical writer, a ballroom dance instructor, a concert promoter, and a marketing director for companies that design schools, libraries, and skateboard parks. Like the Five Ancestors, Mr. Stone was adopted as an infant. He began searching for his birth mother when he was eighteen and found her fifteen years later. *Tiger* is his first novel.